# BENEATH THE STATUE

# BENEATH THE STATUE

## JEREMY COLANGELO

INANNA
CANADA

**Library and Archives Canada Cataloguing in Publication**

Title: Beneath the statue / Jeremy Colangelo.

Names: Colangelo, Jeremy, 1990– author.

Description: Short stories.

Identifiers: Canadiana 20200256262 | ISBN 9781989689103 (softcover)

Classification: LCC PS8605.O3794 B46 2020 | DDC C813/.6—dc23

Printed and bound in Canada on 100% recycled paper.

**Now Or Never Publishing**
901, 163 Street
Surrey, British Columbia
Canada V4A 9T8

**nonpublishing.com**
*Fighting Words.*

We gratefully acknowledge the support of the Canada Council for the Arts
and the British Columbia Arts Council for our publishing program.

# TABLE OF CONTENTS

# THE FOREVER PIT

It was an early morning in June when Alfred Arnold, a sanitation engineer for the Helheim Digging Company, fell into a deep pit. He had slipped on the edge, and off the edge, and as he fell he began to scream. But after an hour his throat was burning and soon he decided to stop. He was a good worker, a dignified man; to uncontrollably scream at such a triviality was beneath him.

The pit was very deep. A machine was making it, and it went nearly forever. They tried to make a forever pit, the digging company, as their organization's crowning achievement (for no digging company had ever made one before), but they hadn't quite yet. The exact depth was very close to infinity—infinity -1 if you like—and still, at the bottom, the machine is digging.

Alfred tried to climb back up, but the pit's walls were too smooth to hold. He decided that it was impossible, but sometimes he would try again. It was like a weekly mid-life crisis.

Poor Alfred, he knew all about the pit. His union had told him everything while they struck the year before. They were trying to get safety rails. Oh well.

So Alfred knew that he would fall until he died. He tried starving to death, to avoid the "*Splat!*" at the end, but he couldn't make himself. People liked to throw things down the hole, bits of their lunch, their scraps. Alfred, you see, had to wear heavy weighted clothing as part of his job, which involved jumping into fluid tanks to fix clogged pipes. Most of the fluids were very dense, like molasses, so most people were too light and couldn't dive. There was depilated uranium woven into his clothing to keep him at the bottom. Alfred, then, had a lot of inertia, so he fell faster than almost everything else, had a higher terminal velocity. The food was old by the time he reached it, but still safe to eat. It was the preservatives.

Other people had fallen down the pit too. One day, Alfred met Angela. This was a few years later. Angela had come to the factory for "take your kid to work day" and had slipped. The company paid her father a small settlement and transferred him to Iceland—which had been best for everyone. Angela was twelve when she fell, and now she was thirty. She wasn't wearing weighted clothing, so she fell much more slowly than Alfred. A bag of marbles in her pocket kept her going fast enough to catch food. Alfred gave her his shirt so they'd fall at about the same speed. When they were bored, they made love like eagles.

Anton was born soon after. It became hard to feed three people and Anton was always bored. Thankfully, someone had dropped a case of books and a puppy down the pit. Alfred and Angela read the books, and little Anton rode the puppy's skeleton like a rocking horse. When Annette was born, he had trouble sharing with her. Luckily they found a dead cat. Now the girl had a toy too. But they were still hungry.

Alfred began sneaking away some of his food during meals and hiding it in a hole in the book case. When Angela went to sleep, he gave it to the kids. Angela didn't like it, she wanted everyone to get enough food and had set strict rations—she was smart like that. But the children loved their daddy, and he loved them too. That's why he starved to death, for love.

Everyone was very sad, especially Angela. They took the weighted clothing off of Alfred's body and let it fly upwards. He hit a discarded propane tank and burst into flames. A Viking funeral.

The children were eight and four. Everyone missed their father still, though he had been dead for a year by then. At bed time, Angela would tell stories of the surface. She taught Anton to read with the books from the shelf. Baby Annette tried to eat one. She bit off a chunk and choked to death. Another funeral. They sent her up with the cat.

It was just the two now, mother and son. Anton was a clever little boy. He said that he didn't believe in his mother's surface stories. They were just to keep him from misbehaving. Those horrid tales of work and school, capitalism and booster shots, none were real. He was a very smart boy, but he was also very not.

They had an argument, Anton and Angela. Anton was twenty by then. He decided to go off on his own. He found an iron spike that had once been part of a threshing machine and jammed it into the wall. His fall slowed, and his mother was soon deep below him. Depressed, she stopped eating and removed her weights, and Anton saw her corpse fly by a few weeks later.

Anton was alone. He flew down the deep pit and thought many lonely thoughts. He wondered about the pit. Was it a god? Was it the belly of a worm? Was it his fears and hates made manifest? What of the food? Who gave it to them? Men dropping strange and random things into a dark hole, or manna from the unseen sky?

Anton thought still more thoughts. He found an empty notebook and a pen and he wrote his ideas down. When he was finished, he let it fly above him. Maybe someone would find it?

Anton never saw anyone else. He lived to one-hundred-and-eight years old and didn't see a single other human being. Anton could have lived forever. Or, at least, forever -1. Philosophers always live a long time. But then something happened that Anton never expected, a singular event which pre-empted his long and fruitful life.

Anton hit the bottom.

## Once Again

And so despite the weakness that sat upon her chest and arms, Prisoner Six began cutting away at the mortar between the stone blocks in the far wall with the edge of the servant's spoon. And each day when she leaned back her head against the wall and breathed exhaustion from her lungs, the pictures in her mind grew weak and her remembrances passed into the void as silver flakes of dust. She could not any longer taste the supper she recalled, nor see again the scars the light carved on her eyes. And so the eye inside her head would jump back weeks or months to a gesture or a word the servant made, which by its strangeness anchored that whole day inside a crevice at the base of Six's skull, and which now stood alone and upright as a nail. She sat crosslegged on the floor and felt her mind fall out from under her, into a dark and empty shaft. And then she would again rise up and dig.

Six never slept, and as far as she recalled had never woken up.

"At least you know what you're doing," said the servant. Six by then had worn a canyon through the mortar in the wall.

"I do?" said Six.

"I must have mentioned that the wall across from the door was the thinnest." The servant gestured with a ladle. She was standing at the open door, which let in a blinding light. "Though, I should reiterate, because it's safe to assume that I've said this before, that there is no way that you'll escape this place. You might have assumed that the wall you're defacing is only as thick as that one stone. I am sorry if I led you to that conclusion. It was unfair of me."

"This is the thinnest wall?"

"Certainly, not including the doorway of course. And the back wall also has the advantage of leading outside. The rest will just send you into the other cells."

"There are—"

"Do you think that I would be able to sustain myself off of just one prisoner in just one cell, master Narcissus?"

"I didn't mean—"

"Just because you can't hear them doesn't mean they aren't there, and anyway you wouldn't *want* to hear them. Frankly, I much prefer *our* talks together—when they occur."

"So," and Six's mind started doing calculations, "you bring me food every two hours, and I assume that the others have to eat as much as I do, and—have we had this conversation before?"

"Probably."

"And they actually do have to eat as much as I do?"

"Indeed."

"And how many of you are there?"

"There is only room for one of me."

"So then the prison must be very small. How many people could you possibly handle in two hours? Especially given how long we chat sometimes."

"There are always enough of you for my purposes, and I am always on time. You must not assume so much."

The servant put down the tray and ladled out the soup. She had a fresh spoon with her, which she left.

"Thank you," said Six.

"The food is my duty."

"I meant for the spoon."

"You need a spoon to eat the food, and the old one is bent."

"..."

"What?"

"I only chose that spot because the mortar had a crack in it. It's been there, the crack, as long as I can remember, and I figured that it would make my life easier to start at a weak spot." The servant smiled, showing no teeth. "What?"

"It is amusing," said the servant, "if I may be so bold, that you would arrange a task of this magnitude around such a minimal convenience."

"Should I have begun with the solid rock?"

"Perhaps not."

The servant collected the old plate from its usual spot and left, as she usually did, before Six could begin eating. The closing door sprayed dark across the wall.

Two hours later, when the servant returned, she brought Six a chisel and hammer.

★

The servant had perhaps not expected Six to remain working without rest. Though each time she brought the food the servant found Six at work, she never said to stop. How many bricks could there be after the first one? Six had nothing else to do in that cell but work. The dark sustained her. Only hunger slowed her down. And yet the servant still continued to bring food. Six would make it through the wall eventually, given time enough.

Six wedged the chisel in the crack above the block and began to pull. The brick slid slowly until it came close to tipping over. It fell out. In the dark Six could not see what was beyond. Her fingers touched out to the back of the hole. The stone was without blemish. Then a bright light from the doorway revealed to Six a solid wall, grey and mercilessly smooth.

"Perhaps you could make yourself a bigger cell," the servant said.

"I—what?"

"I'll pull out that block for you, to keep the room uncluttered. If you remove the rest of the blocks then your room will be much larger. Would that be beneficial?"

"I think so."

"And the floor, the ceiling, the other walls—"

"I'd miss the bumps."

"What?"

"The bumps from the blocks on the floor, the seams, and on the walls when I lean on them—they'd be gone. The room would be completely smooth."

"I suppose it would be. Soup?"

"Is it?"

"Have you gotten sick of soup?"

"What did you bring me last time?"

"You should be more specific."

"What did you bring to this cell two hours ago? I remember eating chicken at some point—chicken breast and something with tomatoes in it."

"Two hours ago in this cell: soup. Previous time: soup. The time before that: soup."

"Are you sure?"

"It may have always been soup, or it may have been soup for a long time now. I suppose it is possible, statistically, if you go long enough—"

"What?"

"You are hungry."

"Yes."

"Had you forgotten?"

"I knew I was hungry before you told me."

"Of course."

"But," Six looked at the doorway, set in walls only two blocks thick, "could I remove the blocks from that wall too?" She pointed.

"From the wall with the door in it?"

"Yes."

"In principle."

"Would you stop me? Or call the guards?"

"The guards?"

"Have we talked about this before?"

"Probably. There are no guards. I am here alone with you."

"And all the prisoners."

"Exactly."

"So why then could I not just overpower you? You are shorter than I am, though I get smaller every time I check. How long until I shrink into a dustmote, subatomic, with all this hunger?"

"It has yet to happen. How long have you been shrinking?"

"Since."

"Since?"

"Since I have been checking, that I remember, I have become thinner and shorter every time. I hold myself against the wall and count the widths of my fingers from the seam above my head. Perhaps I should attack you now before I lose too much of me."

The servant put the tray and soup pot on the stone and took Six's hand. The servant's skin was cold, and her hand felt fat and empty.

"I would rather you just left," the servant said. "It would make my life much easier."

Six didn't move until the servant pulled her hand. At the tug she took two slow steps forward, towards the light in the door. Her pupils closed to needlepoints against the light. The servant released Six's hand and pushed her on the shoulder. Six stepped outside the cell.

★

Her fingers touched out to the back of the hole. The stone was without blemish. Then a bright light from the doorway revealed to Six a solid wall, grey and mercilessly smooth.

"Perhaps you could make yourself a bigger cell," the servant said.

"I—what?"

"I'll pull out that block for you, to keep the room uncluttered. If you remove the rest of the blocks then your room will be much larger. Would that be beneficial?"

"I think so."

"And the floor, the ceiling, the other walls—"

"I'd miss the bumps."

"What?"

"The bumps from the blocks on the floor, the seams, and on the walls when I lean on them—they'd be gone. The room would be completely smooth."

"I suppose it would be. Chicken breast?"

"Is that what you have today? Not soup like usual?"

"It is a bad idea to eat the same thing too many times in a row. Makes people unruly, violent."

"Violent?"

"But you are not violent today—are you?"

"I don't think so."

"Good. I have chicken breast for you, with some tomatoes. Fried."

The servant put the tray on the floor in the middle of the cell. She then placed both hands on the stone and dragged it noiselessly out the door. Six began to eat. The tomatoes burst their guts across her tongue.

★

It was not hard for Six to make a crack along the flat face of the wall. Once she had made a divot in the stone, she began chipping systematically across the face of the rock until the wall was rough and eager for her touch. While she did this, Six decided that the tunnel should angle upwards, since she could get more leverage with the hammer that way.

Digging, Six became like a diver caught at the bottom of the sea, reaching futilely towards the onionskin that sat between the ocean and the sky. She still dug in little forward bursts, and when she struck the stone she imagined that each stonechip she removed was that final scrape of flesh that kept the sky away. But then she would remember that her chisel could get stuck, and she would stop the forward reaching so that she could carve the tunnel wide. Expand her little universe. Somehow, even when she aimed away from the outside, she still expected that each strike would make the light shine through.

At least if she could see the outside then she would be able to judge how long it would take for her to reach it. If she knew, she would be able to forget about the time; she could stop counting the blows against the stone in rhythm with the pulse inside her head, and could forget to listen for the servant's call to eat.

Two hours in between each meal. She had forgotten what two hours felt like until the day her tunnel moved up far enough that the light from the open door no longer reached her. The servant never shouted, so even if she called Six would not have heard her above the noises of the chisel on the rock. But Six could keep the time by her hunger, sometimes getting to the bottom of the tunnel just as the servant closed the door. Six could find the food by smell, once she snorted out the dust. Eventually Six began to miss their talks, and so she learned the rhythms of starvation so to anticipate the visit by the tightening of her gut.

When next the servant came, Six skidded down the shaft and shot straight out the hole. She approached the servant with a scraped-up elbow trickling blood across her arm, her hunger blocking out the pain and all her other thoughts as well.

★

"How goes the excavation?" said the servant.

"Upward."

"Outward?"

"Maybe."

"Maybe."

"Chicken again?"

"Is it again?"

"You remember more than I do."

"But I have more to forget as well."

The servant left the food outside the door and went into the cell to collect the bits of stone that had fallen from the tunnel. A breeze came in from the doorway. When Six blinked she saw red blotches floating passed her, burned there by the light. But Six did not look away.

"You know better than to run," the servant said.

"I would not be able to outpace you," said Six.

"You know that isn't true. I am far too large."

The servant's black shirt and overalls strained against her flesh. She was not fat, but rather seemed like she would be too big no matter what size she was. Was this the first time that Six had noticed? She could not remember.

"What do you eat?" said Six. "No matter how much you feed me, I stay a skeleton. Am I being hungry for two?"

"Have I not told you about this before?"

"Probably."

"Probably." The servant reached outside the cell and grabbed a small stool. Six sat cross-legged on the floor. "I should have known from your voice that you were among those still permitted ignorance."

"And what—"

"'—do I not know?' Yes, that is exactly what happens next. And then I usually tell one of my parables."

"You—"

"Yes."

"But—"

"Because there is always a small chance that a parable will help you learn your place in this little cosmos before you actually try to escape. At least that's what I always tell you."

"But the—"

"Tunnel, yes. I suppose you're right. And usually at this point I talk about who wrote the parables, or how I came to learn them, or why I keep telling them despite it never working before."

"And how many—"

"I don't remember. Have you ever tried to play the lottery? I already know you haven't, but this game works better as a dialogue."

"I—"

"Just say 'no.'"

Six did.

"Good. Well, you know how they work right? Where you have to pick one set of numbers out of an immense quantity of possible combinations, and you only win if the set you picked comes up randomly?"

"Yes."

"Excellent. The way this parable goes is that there is a woman, who I'll call Josephine, who decides that she wants to win the lottery. She picks a set of numbers, which serve her faithfully through several weeks of loss. Eventually she notices that the winning numbers have been equally consistent—identical each week. Josephine starts watching the numbers as they are chosen.

She sits close to her television to make sure that the gentleman who runs the machine that picks the numbered balls has not manipulated the result. She talks to others who play the same lottery to see if they have noticed too, but none of them remember anything about each winning set except that it was not the one that they had picked.

"At first, Josephine is afraid change her numbers, which have been constant for so long now that the time before the lottery has faded in her mind. 'They are random, right?' she says. 'They are chosen from the machine. I see it roll around filled with balls with numbers on them, and I see the little tube that each ball is sucked into. Which numbers come up still depends on how they bounce around inside the machine. Physics. But I can at least treat it like it's random. And that means that there is no guarantee that next week the numbers will be the same.'

"This is what Josephine tells herself every week, until one time as an experiment she decides to change. As she goes up to purchase her ticket, she expects that the cashier will give her a surprised look, as if he had just caught her cheating. But, of course, he has no idea which numbers she has bought, and may not even remember her. After all, who knows what the cashier does when Josephine is gone?

"Josephine takes the tickets and she waits until the numbers appear, and they are the same ones that have come up every week before. Josephine has finally won the lottery. Rich beyond reasoning and duly satisfied, she stops playing for a while, but then, probably by chance, she checks the numbers again, and finds that they are still the same. She knows that her friends still play their old numbers, that they will continue to lose the game and so increase the jackpot every week. She buys another ticket, and wins the lottery again. Then another week goes buy and she wins a third time, and then a fourth. Soon Josephine forgets the taste of hunger.

"Now the whole country knows that Josephine is rich—that she is perhaps Fortuna, god of luck. And so she continues to buy the same numbers every week, and continues to win and revel, and continues to watch the other players lose. But sometimes

Josephine remembers that she has no idea what goes on inside of the machine, that as far as she's concerned the numbers are random. So every so often Josephine goes to cast her old standby, not hoping that she'll win, but that she will lose in a way that she has not before. But, as far as I remember, this has not occurred.

"So now, old friend," the servant said, "it is time you told me a story. When did you begin to dig that tunnel in the wall?"

"A while ago," said Six.

"How long is a while?"

"I don't know."

"Do you remember the moment that first tore away the stone?"

"Not really."

"And do you know where the chisel came from?"

"I've had it forever. Haven't I?"

"As far as I'm aware," the servant said, "but I'd like to take it from you."

"No."

"As payment for the food I bring you."

"No!"

"Why not?"

"Because it is mine."

"How?"

"Because I have had it for my whole life—as long as either of us remembers. How can that be true without the chisel being mine?"

"But if you gave it to me, then it would be mine instead."

"Yes."

"And I demand it in exchange for your food."

"You have never asked for it before."

"In all likelihood, I have asked for it many times, and many times you have given it to me. The food you eat is mine to give, or to not give, and I know you need to eat it. The condition has always been, as you recall, that you would give me what I want in exchange for the food I bring, and anything you have is fair for me to ask for. Everything you own is thus already mine."

"I could stop eating," said Six.

"Your death would be merely inconvenient."

"I would give up everything then, so there would be nothing that you could take from me. But—"

"But?"

"All that I own are this chisel, the hammer, and the clothes I wear. What do you take when you have all of those?"

"I might not want to take them all. I can take whatever I like—everything or nothing as I choose."

"But what else is there?"

"That right there is the answer to your question."

"What question."

"Earlier you asked what I eat. The answer is that I eat exactly what I want to eat, and given long enough I will someday want to swallow you."

The servant stood up and slowly pushed the stool out the door with her foot. Six, scraping her knees on the floor, crawled with insect speed towards her hole. The rubble from before was gone, though she hadn't seen the servant carry it away. The smell of charcoal briefly floated through her nose before being pushed back by the chalky dust.

As she lost sight of the cell, Six noticed briefly that her hunger had gone away. But then it returned, with barbs.

"How long is the tunnel?" the servant said. She had not moved from the door.

"What?"

"You have been digging that tunnel for a long time—yes?"

"Yes."

"As long as you remember?"

"Right."

"So it must be very far. I'm surprised that you can still come on time for food. How long is it, exactly?"

"It goes," Six calculated, "up to where the light from the open door disappears behind the curve. A little farther, actually, since there's still room enough after that for the length of my body."

"That isn't far."

"The stone is very hard."

"The stone crumbles in your hand. It's almost talc. You could cut it with a spoon if you wanted to. Clearly that chisel isn't helping."

"But I've been digging for so long."

"And you are so far from the outside edge that the birds have yet to hear the echoes of your hammer through the stone. Come down now—I have food for you."

"You're going to stab me with the chisel!"

"No."

"You'll eat me alive?"

"I am not going to eat you today, and the chance of my eating you tomorrow, or on any given day, is so small as to be almost zero. But everyone has to die eventually."

"And then one day you will stab me with the chisel."

"I want the chisel because the chisel is mine. You will know when the time has come for me to eat you when the food I bring is poisonous."

"You're going to poison my food?"

"Maybe. Not today."

"How do I know that you're not lying?"

"You can trust me. Come down from the tunnel."

"I won't until you—" but then Six's hand shifted. The walls of the tunnel suddenly felt slippery, though they remained rough enough to tear her skin. The first scrape on her elbow had already begun to heal, though now it was torn open again, and at the bottom of the tunnel Six found that the stone of the floor was soft.

"Stand up," the servant said. "I know exactly how it goes— you were going to refuse to eat. You would have said that my argument was futile. You were going to come down from the tunnel on your own and let me bring the food, and then you were going to throw it to the darkness of your cell and let the two hours of eternity devour you as the hunger filled the crannies of your mind." The servant pushed Six down and leered over her. Six, her arm up to guard her face, looked at the servant's eyes and saw no fury in them.

"I don't know what you want me to do," Six said.

"Do you now know how *bored* I am with you? I barely even think about what I say to you anymore. I don't even know what I would do if you were to try something I didn't expect."

Just as the servant spoke, Six stood up and tried to strike her across the face, but the servant barely had to move to avoid the blow.

"But the violence is a part of the machine. Do you know what I do once I poison someone?"

"I don't."

"Maybe I unhinge my jaw and swallow them whole. Or maybe the poison leaves them alive, but paralysed, and I just stand over them as they starve, and I watch the room digest them, and then I cup their liquid bodies in my hands and sip. I feel full for a while, and then suddenly I don't. It's like you barely existed at all."

"That's a lie. Now you're just trying to scare me."

"It doesn't matter. As far as you're concerned, it's as true as the sky above your head—blue and cloudless, last time I checked, and sometimes there are birds."

With great unbalance, Six pulled back her hand again, against the spasm in her gut where the numbness had betrayed her, and held the blow above her shoulder while she looked into the servant's depthless eyes, her face made dark by the glare of the hall. Outside the cell her food was waiting.

Two hours later, the servant came again with food, and left as soon as it was placed. Six ate the meal. She felt she had no choice; she knew this was the end.

★

A woman known as Prisoner Six waited inside a cell for her meal. She was thin, dressed in a black smock and covered in a misty haze of grey dust from the walls around her. There were no windows in her cell, and the door shut without a seam, and she could only by the nervetips of her fingers know the edges of the room. Every two hours the servant came bearing food, and so opened the door and let in the light. Six spent the time between the feedings walking in a circle around the cell's perimeter, trying not to think about the time, trailing her fingers across the walls, unblemished except for a thin crack in the mortar across from the door.

One day the servant brought Six soup, and also a metal spoon, and so despite the weakness that had sat upon her chest and arms, Prisoner Six flattened out the spoon against the floor and wedged it in the crack. She slowly began to dig out the mortar, and eventually removed the stone, revealing behind the wall a flat face of solid rock. Six held her ear to the wall, trying to hear birds outside, but she could not.

The servant continued to come on time, and never mentioned the tunnel that Six had begun to dig, though one day she left a chisel and a hammer with the food. Eventually, Six dug a thin passage, sloping upwards, just far enough in that she could no longer see the light of the door when it was time to eat. It was a good thing, then, that this time the servant had brought a lantern with her.

"I have your food." The servant placed the tray on the edge of the tunnel, on the small flat area left by the stone that Six removed, which was by chance just deep enough to fit the tray. Six looked down and saw the servant looking up the tunnel, lantern held in a gloved hand.

"Aren't you going to leave?" said Six.

"I will, eventually."

"Have I asked about this before?"

"Probably. There are many questions in this room, and most of them are yours."

"I am very hungry."

"Then come down and eat."

"With you watching me?"

"Yes."

"Why."

"Because you have to eat, whether I am here or not. You remember that, at least?"

Six thought back as far as she could go. "I do," she said, perhaps with uncertainty.

"Then come down to eat," the servant said, "before that tunnel closes in and traps us all."

# Unconditional Love

"Sweetie, please, you like carrot sticks."

"No I don't."

"Yes you do—you ate them at Grandma's house. You even asked for seconds."

"No I didn't."

"Well I say you did, and now I just want you to eat some more."

"No."

"Just eat five."

"No, Mommy."

"Three, and then I'll let you go play."

"Promise?"

"Promise."

Marie took the carrot sticks and carefully put them in her mouth. When she finished, she called over her mother Eliza, who suddenly found the ceiling fan very interesting.

"There, Mommy."

"What?"

"Three."

"Oh, well, I don't know. I didn't see you eat them. It looks more like one. Eat two more."

"I did too eat them."

"Marie, please don't lie to me."

"Mommy—"

"Marie, stop that right now." Eliza spoke with a voice of cold barbs. "I said eat three and you ate one, you have to keep up your end of our deal. You made a commitment. Now be a big girl and keep your side of the bargain."

"But you—"

"You know there are children in Haiti who would love to eat your carrot sticks. They go all day without food and they don't have mommies like me to take good care of them. Just think about that when you say you want me to waste good food."

"Do they really have to go hungry for a whole day?"

"Yes, sometimes more than one. And they're all just like you, only they aren't as lucky as you were to be born here. Now do you still want me to throw those carrot sticks away?"

Marie said no, and ate each one while her mother watched. When she finished, Marie looked up at Eliza with horrified eyes.

"What is it, Sweetie?"

"Now I ate all the carrots. We should have given some to the kids."

"I—"

"Can we do something to help them, Mommy? I want them to have some carrots too."

"Well, dear, you already ate them all."

"So?"

"We can't do everything for them, dear. We just need to remember them when we think about throwing food away."

"But can we do anything else to help?"

"Uh—yes, I put some money in a donation box the other day. That ought to be enough."

★

An hour later, Eliza and Dan successfully avoided their neighbour's eyes as they buckled Marie in her car-seat. For their own sakes, they remembered to bring along the portable TV to keep their precious little girl from bothering them on the three hour ride. They were exactly twenty-two minutes late. As the car left the subdivision, passing through the iron gate, Dan's memory sparked.

"Eliza, did I forget to lock the door?"

"Yes."

"Really?"

"Yes, Dan, you left it unlocked, and I didn't tell you because I am, on good authority, 'a mirthless cunt'." Eliza did not look up from her book.

"Eliza, the kid—"

"Is wearing headphones."

"But I thought we talked about—"

"You just ran the light."

He had indeed, and when the sirens pulled him over, and Dan saw his reflection in the Officer's shades, Eliza just stared out the windshield at the cars all slowing down as they went by.

"Did you see the light, sir?"

"No I didn't, Officer."

"Why weren't you paying attention?"

"Well, I was."

"So did you see the light?"

"Well, yes, but I was also talking to my wife here and, uh, yah, I was just talking and the light changed, uh, so quickly, but then you see I, uh, we weren't really trying to hurt anyone because—"

"Your licence is expired, sir."

"I—I know."

"So you were knowingly driving with an expired license."

"No. No, I didn't know, and I didn't see the light, and I—"

"Ma'am."

Eliza pushed Dan back in his seat. "Yes, Officer."

"Is your licence up to date?" The Officer handed her the ticket.

"Yes it is."

"And are you able to drive today?"

"But it's my car." Dan barely heard himself.

"I'm alright, Officer," Eliza said.

"Fine then." Dan and Eliza changed places and they waited for the squad car to leave. Dan made sure the TV volume was up.

"What *was* that?"

"We both own this car, Dan." Eliza spoke with a tone of steel wool.

"You just watched me make a damn fool of myself in front of the police."

"We paid for this jointly, Dan."

"And you just smiled at that cop like you were friends or—"

"I drive this car every day—"

"Or lovers or—"

"I drive it for an hour every morning before you even wake up—"

"Or like you both knew the punch-line to a joke and—"

"And you just sit all day and play on your computer—"

"And that is my *job*, Eliza."

"And I go out and do all the damn work—"

"Sure you get to go out and talk to crazy people—"

"I make more money in an hour than you do in a day."

It was right about then that they began to get unreasonable. Eliza pulled on the highway, and was immediately stuck in traffic. After informing Dan of all of the ways that he could go fuck himself, Eliza consoled the crying Marie (who had paid closer attention than they thought) and said that everything was all right and that no, Mommy and Daddy were not having an argument. She then called for an extended moment of silence in honour of her final nerve, which was now very close to expiring.

*

About an hour later, Marie emitted a loud wailing sound—the sort of noise her parents hated more than any other, because it immediately put them at her bidding. Dan, his hair matted with sweat from the broken A/C, turned off her television and asked her what was wrong.

"My tooth hurts," said Marie.

"Where does it hurt?"

"What hurts?" said Eliza.

"My tooth," said Marie.

"Which tooth?" said Dan.

"The back one."

"Which back one?"

"This one here." She pointed somewhere on her cheek.

"Marie, could you open your mouth and let me see?"

"It hurts, Daddy."

"Stop hurting her, Dan," said Eliza.

"I didn't even touch her yet," said Dan. "Marie, can you be more specific?"

"I feel it behind my eyes."

"Are you sure it's not just a headache."

"No."

"Then let me see." He reached back and grabbed her chin. Marie began to cry again. Luckily, the moaning kept her tongue from getting in the way. Eliza, hearing the ruckus, turned to see, but Dan insisted that everything was fine, that he knew what he was doing, and that since Eliza had wanted to drive so much, she should just pay attention to the road and let him take care of the child. Eliza, tired of fighting, decided to let that one go.

"You look fine," said Dan to Marie.

"It hurts."

"Maybe you're just tired."

"It hurts."

"I think you're fine."

"No, Daddy." She pressed her palms against her temples.

"Marie—"

"Help me, Daddy."

"Marie, stop that—"

"Why does my tooth hurt, Daddy?"

"Marie, stop." He held her hands down. "Look at me." She did. "And stop crying." She did. "Now listen, I don't see anything. We brushed your teeth before we left and I saw you floss out all the bits of food. I don't know what's going on, but you do not have a toothache."

"But I do—Mommy—"

"Marie," Eliza said, "if Daddy looked and didn't see anything, then there isn't anything there. Please settle down."

"I'm sorry."

"And I don't want you making a fuss about this tonight," said Dan, "you understand? You have to be a good girl, ok? Can you be a good girl for Daddy?"

"Yes."

"Then no more of this. You do not have a toothache."

"Alright."

"Good girl. I'll put the movie back on."

Dan turned on the television. Marie did not watch it though. Instead she took off her headphones and wrapped her arms around her face, rocking back and forth and trying not to moan. Dan fiddled with his cell phone until the battery died. He had left the charger at home.

★

An hour later—when the pressure had gone down and the boredom had made talking more attractive—they drove past an old man standing outside his car, which had broken down and was now parked on the shoulder. Eliza slowed down just a little bit to get a better look.

"Did you see that guy, Dan?" said Eliza, pointing.

"Hm?" Dan twisted around to see.

"With the shirt and the beard, like a hippie or something."

"Oh really?"

"I mean, honestly, who dresses like that? People should know better."

"Better than what?"

"Better than to go out like that in public. Now I have to look at it."

"Right, right, because if you want to look like that in private—"

"Then that's fine, because no one has to see, but in public—"

"People might get the wrong idea and think you're some kind of—"

"Right, right." Eliza nodded and tapped the steering wheel.

"And that would be bad."

"Of course."

"Because even if I was, hypothetically—"

"Right, like that."

"It wouldn't be right to just go out and make a declaration."
Dan threw up his hands.

"That would be ridiculous."

"So you can be all like—"

"*Like*—"

"That in private if you want, but you have to dress up when
you go out for other people's sake, at the very least. 'There's a
time and a place'."

"Exactly. It's not like I go out wearing my wedding dress or
you go out wearing a tuxedo."

"Who would do that?"

"It's like when you go out on a first date and you dress up
all nice and go out somewhere fancy just to make things feel
special."

"We don't do that in real life."

"No, that would be silly. But you do it then because that's
just what's expected of you."

"It's common courtesy."

"And then the other person knows that you're probably not
like that in real life—"

"Right."

"And so when you go to a wedding, and everyone dresses
up, and you have the priest and the tuxedo and the wedding
dress, and everyone sits all quiet while you all promise to love
each other unconditionally forever and ever."

"Right, all that stuff."

"Well, we all have to do that. And we all know that there's
going to be fights and bickering, but for now let's just pretend that
everything is fine so we can go about our business and get things
done because, really, we are all stuck here together and no one
thinks this is the best way to do things anyhow, and existing in the
world is frankly bullshit sometimes. So if someone makes a fuss
then we'll all have to bring up all the nonsense again—and no one
wants that—and then there will be an argument and I really just
don't want to deal with this right now so if we could all just keep

calm and go along with things and then everything would be nice and quiet and, really, why can't we all just have a nice time like we used to?" Eliza's breath began to pick up. Dan recoiled.

"Are you alright?" he said.

"Yes."

"But are you—"

"Yes, it's fine. It's just that guy really bugged me. I don't want to have an argument."

"Because you know you can tell me anything."

"Dan, I don't want to get into this." She pulled her shoulders in.

"Alright, I just—"

"Please just stop, ok? I just don't want to have this discussion."

★

After the loving couple stepped out of their minivan, and pulled their docile and obedient charge out of her seat, they walked (holding hands) up the concrete steps and on to the front porch where they waited—politely—for the door to open. Inside, scattered on the cushy chairs and couches, was their extended family—chatting about this and that. Dan put his car keys on an end table, and with Eliza and Marie stood courteously, leaning on the banister and edging their way into the conversation. They stood patiently until the uncle with the big ears (was it Uncle Kevin, or Uncle Mike?) stood up from the sofa to use the bathroom. By the uncle's return, Dan and Eliza had already usurped his empty spot with Marie on their laps. The uncle, seeing this, only nodded and sat on the floor—keeping an eye on one of his brothers in-law, who had just finished his fourth beer on a notoriously small bladder.

"So, how old are you now?" It was Aunt Clarissa, with whom Dan and Eliza shared the couch.

"Six," said Marie holding up six finders, "but going on seven—so I guess I'm more like six-and-a-half," she lifted another half-way. Eliza and Dan laughed, and Marie lowered her hands. Her tooth was still bothering her, and she tried to get down for a glass of ice water, but Eliza held her in place.

You are going to *be social*—Eliza would have said if she'd needed to—I don't want you to embarrass me.

"That is very big for a little girl like you," said Aunt Clarissa, "and you've gotten so tall. Have you been eating all your vegetables?"

"We try to get her to, but she—" but Dan suddenly realised that no one was listening to him.

"I do, I guess, but I don't think I should," said Marie.

"And why not?"

"Well, Mommy said that some poor people in a bad place need the food too. Shouldn't I give my carrots to them?"

"I, oh—"

"Marie," said Eliza, "you stop that right now."

"But Mommy—"

"We are having a good time here. You are being impolite." She turned to Aunt Clarissa. "I'm sorry about her."

"Oh I know. She was so nice last time." Aunt Clarissa decided not to notice Eliza letting Marie get away. The two women started talking—but later on neither could remember what they had said. When a voice called from the kitchen asking if anyone would have a drink, they both answered yes.

Meanwhile, Marie had gotten her glass of water—which tasted like the bit of carrot hidden underneath her gum—and had gone under the kitchen table to escape the adults. All the noise and all the being social had made her head feel full. There wasn't anything for her to do, no other children yet, no toys, no pets. Why did her parents bring her here? Outside it was still sunny, and the front door was open. Obviously someone would notice her if she tried to go outside; of course someone would worry if she disappeared. Her parents did notice she was gone once the food was all laid out and the kids' table stayed empty, but by then Marie had already gone two blocks and had forgotten to remember the way back.

★

Of course they found her—once they knew she was gone and had spread out across the neighbourhood, it did not take much time at all. It had been Eliza, driving the familiar van, who had brought her home. Ever afraid of strangers, Marie had avoided the other cars and ran away when she heard people call her name. Dan had wanted to take the car, but he couldn't drive without a licence. He had walked three kilometres in the wrong direction before Aunt Clarissa found him and brought him back.

So that was it for the dinner. None of the other family members talked to Marie after that, and Eliza would not let go of her hand. What had the poor girl been thinking? You simply didn't do that to people—running off out of boredom, not saying where you were. They asked her what she'd been thinking, and she said she didn't know. They said she *had* to know, she *had* to remember. What kind of kid was this?

Marie, Eliza, and Dan were the first to leave that night. They left early because of the long drive—they said—and not for any other reason at all. But the night had been hard on them. Ten minutes away from the house, Eliza stopped the car and stepped outside to think and get some air. Dan rubbed his forehead and asked Marie to please not talk for a while.

A family of four drove by just about then, bored and tired and desperate to get home. They saw Eliza outside—her hair frizzy with sweat and stress, and her breath coming out white with cold. ("Or is that a cigarette? And with a *child* in the car!") People like that shouldn't have children—they all agreed—people *like that*, so irresponsible. Can't you at least try to look presentable? What kind of example is are you setting? What kind of mother goes around stopping her car on a busy highway to smoke? And with her hair all frizzed up like some kind of hippie.

"Don't ever let me catch you looking like *that*," said the mother to her daughter. "It just isn't proper."

The daughter nodded, and said that she would not.

"Good girl," the mother said.

## THE IMAGES

After the war came the returning, when ghosts fell from their images and drew about gravely the streets. It was about then that I and Arthur went out to find a photograph, which had gone missing from the shrine outside the post office near the centre of town.

As happens, the people who remained from war set up a meeting place. Once the newspapers and world claimed the war had ended, they put up photographs of their young ones who had gone away, asking—has anybody seen them? You become a different person, it was said, in the trenches, in the burnt out cities, fighting room to room in the cold and dark like venom. You forget that not all assemblages of bodies are a graveyard, that time exists outside the rending of the world, that the cracking of a bullet and the patter of the rain are different sounds. Unrecognizable. And yet your face will stay the same, even when the figure under it has not, even when a changeling has come down to settle on your soul. There remains, I learned, a chance that someone will recognize you, even when you cannot recognize yourself.

After some months of returnings, hope began to whither on the faces on the bulletin board. The meeting place became a shrine, for worship of the lostness pantheistic everywhere. Photos grew like scars over the board, more of them, it seemed, than there were ever people in the town. All about the country the wilderness had grown into a city of the dead, stones had paved the fields and there was no place you could go not rotten with a name. Encrypted mournerless engravings lay about, polluting all our memories. Wood for the coffins ran out and the abundance, the overabundance, of the loss began to overflow. Nostalgia laid upon our beds and ate our food, squatted at our doorsteps, loafed and took up space in all our rooms, making vagrants of us even in our homes.

Once or twice back in the beginning a soldier would return and, no longer being lost, their face would vanish from the board. One day you would see them, set and sturdy pinned up where they'd always been, and the next day like a ghost they'd be before you, real. It was always strange and startling to recall that these lost people could exist. For nowadays you were just as likely to encounter the live cadaver of the memory, the person who was once among you ambling on without their body, just a displaced presence that had tried to fill-in for a void. They shuffled without solemnness, ghoul-like in their normalcy.

I ought to say that these were not shades of the dead that wandered among us, for sometimes the person who'd replaced them was still alive. It's true—one day we all saw it, when a young woman who we all could have sworn went off in uniform just years ago stepped out to the shrine, just like you do, to place a candle and to say a little prayer, when all of a sudden *she* showed up, a spectral woman out of time, the real thing back at last. She didn't seem to notice herself over by the candles when she stepped over the line to the bulletin board and pulled her photo from its pin, held it up for us to see and—smiled? I'd say that's what she tried to do. In any case, as you'd expect, the next day there was only one of those women left in town. Her singularity came as a relief; it returned an almost quiet to us. That's why I and Arthur had to go out looking when the photo disappeared.

But I guess by now we're used to having two of things. At one point it felt good to have a war, like how it feels good to stretch your arms out in the morning. But once it got going they needed to come up with a reason. At first they told us it would keep us safe, which I remember made sense at the time. But when the first of us came back with their joy and feeling hollowed out, came back with their limbs torn off, came back and brought disease, all the old reasons were forgot and the truth naturally presented itself. We discovered we were fighting for revenge, against the people who did these things to us during the war that they, in turn, were also fighting for revenge.

Et cetera occurred until the war was over, which was to say until the war felt sufficiently over to convince ourselves that it was. Arthur, for example, says that from his point of view it seems the war continues, that it will always continue, though not always in the same way. Pockets of warring congregate here and there, like weather systems, and always in or near the villages, always in the places people forget. Arthur said that for him being at war was the natural state of existence, so it made sense that when people forgot to not be at war they would quickly return to it again, that peace for him was like a spring held shut. Whereas I said not being at war was like not thinking about the sun. Most of the time when you're thinking about something you're not thinking about the sun, but then when someone starts talking about not thinking about the sun, or when by chance you glass up and start to notice your surroundings, suddenly you're thrown back into thinking about it—until one day you start thinking about other things again without even noticing that something changed. Arthur pointed out that if that were the case, then the moment you noticed you were not at war it would suddenly be like you were at war again, which I said I guess is true.

At the shrine, a worshipper cried pleading at the icon of a young man sharply dressed in an officer's uniform. I had seen the man standing behind her in line at the grocery store just yesterday, he not noticing her at all, she pretending not to notice but so obviously stung.

Part of the problem is that, when the war is everywhere, when time and space are the same thing, and with memory being what it is, it was not as though the people who went away could all simply arrive home at the same time. There was a train station in the city but the returners never used it, nor did they use the roads. But also they did not just manifest to being somewhere near their photograph, as if pre-made for existence. They did arrive, did in fact traverse to some extent, and in many cases two of them would claim to have left the battlefield at the same time and arrived in town at the same time, when clearly one had been back for a year or more when the second one appeared.

I asked Arthur what he thought and he said it was a mystery.

This all brings me to the manner in which we found the photograph, which was curious. You see an elderly man, a drifter, had stolen it, just tore it off its pin and had begun parading it about the town bellowing nonsense.

"You see!" he said when we came upon him, following his noise. "Look!" he pointed at us. "There, the two of them! I swear to you!" A police officer, cold and tighteyed, her vision scanning through and over us, stood before him.

"Sir," she said, "enough of this. You must come with me."

She took the man by the arm. Hazily, his eyes scorched over decades ago by mustard gas, the old man let himself be guided down the street, the image falling defeated from his hands.

Arthur picked it up. He turned to me. Around him I saw the world begin to cringe, as though space itself were making a mistake.

I stepped forward, holding my hand on his shoulder, holding my hand out, his hand out, holding the photograph, holding out my hand as though at nothing, holding out my hand and there was the green sleeve of a uniform, holding out my hand and holding my own shoulder, holding myself steady by the arm.

I was alone in the village square pulling my own photo from the shrine and the streets were empty and full of people and nobody spoke or saw or touched. Far in the distance I saw a child with his mother, walking. With the photo in my hand I waved, a photo of me waving waving in my hand which also waved. And then the child waved as well.

# Note on Filicide

A professor of psychology, dissatisfied with Stanley Milgram's work, his famous experiment on the interpretation of authority, decides that she can do better. She hires an actor to lay tied and blindfolded on a table, hooks him up with what he thinks are fake electrodes, and attaches the whole mechanism to an array of sensors to detect any gaze that may be pointed in his direction. She hires four students to sit and stare at him as the current slowly every moment rises. They have all been told that this is fake, have been briefed extensively on Milgram's trickery, and have been told as well that the test is meant to see how long they can remain inside the room amid the actor's feigned distress. They are told too about the sensors, and how the experiment will end once there are no watchers in the room. Their compensation will be pegged to the length of time they last inside. As the experiment begins, the actor quickly learns that the electrodes are real, but of course his cries for help are passed off as clever acting, the growing pool of urine just the dedication of a master of the art. But slowly the smell of burning skin becomes too compelling, the spasms in his limbs too violent to be fake, and each subject starts to fear the absence of disgust, the easy way the professor goaded them into this spectacle. They file from the room—one, two, three, four—and so the actor is left writhing on the table amid the constant shocks of pain, the melting of his flesh beneath the heat. *But are the eyes not gone?* the actor thinks, just as his heart gives out. The current remains on for just a moment more, cutting off just as the final watcher turns away.

## LAPIDARY EYES

Madeline was busy loitering in the National Galley when she noticed a candle floating at the edge of her eye, its lapis tonguetip lapping at her lashes with its glow. For a second, nearly, Madeline was still. But then she blinked, and then the candle disappeared, replaced by a small man in a white shirt whose blue and glowing cellphone screen was far too bright. Behind him, Holbein's *The Ambassadors*, its white *memento mori* drawing tourists to its edge.

Madeline went home that night and forgot the candle and the beauty of its lie. But the blue sheen and its curvature still gripped, forming in her dreams a great and undulating monster, carved by mind and vision into faces, hands, and teeth. And then, just when the monster grasped her, the borderlands would shift and those bent features would become a smiling, friendly face.

It was at breakfast, over tea, that the memory came over her, feasting on the air, extinguishing her other thoughts like candles in a glass. There is no obsession like the artist's, driven by hallucinations real enough to bend the flesh of stone, the forces of the sea, the endless depths of language—all to birth a small and pitiful ekphrasis of their dreams. The lonely punctum of the vision, its singularity, the perfect specificity of its truth, thinned the scope of Madeleine's eyes, sapping her peripheries until only its faint light appeared. Plans were drawn, paints procured, her other projects all forgotten, lost in a messy heap as she cleared the studio for space.

The falsehood of the eye is its perfection. Its image, when directly looked upon, is so much itself, so good a figure of reality, that we mistake the phantom for the flesh. The problem was to show the blur on canvas, to make a habitat for her discovery so that the guests may get a sense of what the world is like.

Thankfully the vision granted its unmaking, though it led Madeline through dark and pathless woods. At the edges were a mist, carved at intervals by the flutters of the eye. It was the rough gem, not its point of vanishing, that Madeline desired. And through her hundred ruined paintings she pursued it, layering at first above and then below her images the thinnest paints, the rarest shades, the bright and then the dark, until a year went by and she'd produced a great curved manifold of twisting ultramarine—its magnificence of its blue wash concealing lines and patterns complex as the eyes with which they would be seen.

The night before the debut, Madeline took one last chance to calibrate her work. In the dim light of the closed museum she paced from wall to wall to floor, shifting gently the marker of the spot where she would have the viewer stand, raising first then lowering the circle on the far wall where the eye would fix to hold the painting at its skirt.

It was a moment that would last a thousand years. For a century and more thereafter the historians would work, scanning the remains of Madeline's beatific corpse. Her height and gait, her posture, and most importantly the shape and structure of her eyes, modeling with increased precision, deploying at each chance the latest simulations to acquire the gaze that just that once had held perfection at its edge. Perhaps one in a hundred thousand had from birth the tools with which she carved her morass into art, but with time they would reclaim the painting's fixity and put front and center the artwork as it truly was, with all the beauty that its maker had intended years and years ago. With their minds they shaped another Madeline from clay, and then gave her vision to the world.

The canvas is too old now for the sun. But its image—but its truth—has been set free. Captured after years of work, released now on a shirt, now on a coffee mug, a smiling face of deepest candle blue, whose eyes (if looked at right) betray the slight but immanent eruption of a scream.

# LIVING ARRANGEMENTS

Lying here in bed just so, just as a body restless lies just so, I lay my pen upon this page. People, though not the few people who know me, still react with shock, horror even, when I tell them how many books I wrote longhand. But the swirling specificity of the pen I think reflects the specificity of the dream, and the dream I bridge cannot live in the cursory inscribings of a keyboard which presses samey shapes and samey letters to the page. It wasn't good for T, not even "not good enough", just not good, and not good enough for that matter for Jaunty. Given recent events I would not say it isn't good enough for me, but God knows I am due for a luxury.

I mean good enough for the memoire. This memoire. Which is what I'm calling it for now.

The autobiography of a writer is due great suspicion, not so much for lies as for embellishments. Dream entangles so great a part of our lives that we dare not live without it, nor even go outside if it can be avoided. What is there to describe but hours at a desk, days in blackened reverie—precisely those things which words are forbidden to describe. Language is movement. A sentence is a thing in motion: a bullet creature, noun that bursts from verb. Stasis is an abomination, yet that's what writing *is*.

California, my caretaker, says my subject matter, my writing books for children, is what makes my dream so potent, since the young alone can see the real behind the unreal of the world—or however the saying goes. But I doubt. A doubter, I am always doubting. My nature it is, I think. The books, the *Jaunty's Japes and Jingles* series, had, not so much a formula, more of an equation. Formula actually sounds better. Jaunty was a scampy, wry-eyed, messy-headed, stripling of a boy who lived, lives, in a junkyard and goes about his small midwestern town playing pranks and jokes. At first on the locals, and then on a rotating and expanding cast of outsiders—businessmen, politicians, FBI agents, travelling salesmen, cultists, a circus, and so on.

The point was never to be mean spirited, though many saw Jaunty and his band of friends that way. Each prank was an attempt to help the victim see the world in a new way, or to express some possibility that was always there but never seen. For example, in *Jaunty the Jabberer* Jaunty meets a new teacher who comes to work in his small one-room school. She eventually became a regular character, but at the time I invented her the idea was that when she got driven out of town at the end she would stay that way. You see, Jaunty got the idea, I have no idea where, that a talkative, lively classroom would make the young lady feel welcome. He always found silences awkward, you see, alienating might be a better word, and his fear of the quiet and inability to really "get" that other people are other people were always chief aspects of his character. In any case, I don't want to spoil it, but things eventually worked out that the teacher came around to Jaunty's point of view and eventually started promoting classroom loudness in other schools and parroting some of Jaunty's big ideas. At the time, readers complained that all my characters would start distinct and different but then after a book or two would become exactly like Jaunty. And so what if that's true—to a certain extent? That was the great strength of Jaunty as a protagonist, the way he floated like a vapour through the works, filling every container he was put in like a vision fills the head.

My last book with Jaunty—oh maybe twenty years ago, thirty now perhaps—never got published save in a small run that was quickly remaindered. I think I have a few author copies somewhere in the estate (for all the use that does me) and California still has her signed first edition that she says she reads out every night, but it seems that people just weren't ready to be taken-in by Jaunty, just like the other characters he pranked. I realized while I was writing *Jaunty's Jeopardy* and the books leading up to it that a character was just a set of words and notions that a person put a name to, and that words were just another way of letting dream step out to your brainspace for a second, which is really all it needs. Words are floaty squiggly things that we take to have fixed meanings, yet they could not be more strange. Words are a prank, is what I'm saying, a big joke that our brains play on us, and all I did with *Jaunty's Jeopardy* is let people realize they'd been had.

T said later that you don't do that, for the same reason you don't tell a fish it's sushi, but T appreciated me for what I was and said that since I wouldn't be writing books again after the incident and anyway had California to look after me that it might make sense for me to pull things back for just a while. That is a lie—T never "said" anything. T willed that I would know T's will, and so I did.

By T I mean of course *there*, *their*, and *they're*, each of which describe T perfectly, though not quite all the way. I decided to collapse them into a kind of nickname, and T never told me to stop.

People have said over time that my output scorched my brain and gave me burnout. They said, "Pricilla Noctis publishes something like four children's books a year and does readings and signings and interviews on television and reviews new books in the *Times*—no wonder she went down the way she did. No wonder she got depressed all the time. The woman was burning the candle from four ends at once!"

And while all of this is true I think it misunderstands the real reason for work, for *the* work. You see when I get into a book, usually one I'm writing, it's like the universe has died within my head. I empty out quite totally, as though I have ceased to exist, to occupy space. No, that isn't right. When I work it is as though I am become the space I occupy, that I am not a body seated at a desk and a hand holding a pen, that I am not *beside* this stack of magazines or *beneath* this mold stain in the ceiling, I am not *among* the dust and trash of the room. I have no relation to them because relation presupposes a perspective, a point of view. But in the reverie of writing I abandon the points from which I view, the fact and placement of my body, and from that vanishment the work emerges as though it were the mere detritus of a dream. I awaken to see Jaunty fixed upon a page, his name and presence twisted into letters—trapped and legible, and screaming.

I suppose then that's why it took me so long to get around to memoires, why I do it now these decades after my name has fallen from the lips of my readers for the last time. I needed to pay penance, to T and to Jaunty and to California in a way, by fixing myself between the margins like I had fixed all them. I must write without abandoning myself, and let me tell you that ain't fun.

At times like this I remember my heyday, when T's visions did not seem to friendly as they do today, back when I had only met Jaunty and didn't quite know him. My early books were quite successful, though not to the extant of my middle period, and with all the money I took in I purchased a grand estate house on a vineyard some miles outside Pasadena. The vines I leased out to another winery, since I wanted them for the scenery more than anything else, on the condition that I have a private road through the woods to get on and off my property and that they never, ever step inside my home. For the most part even to this day the now-owners of the land around my house have kept their end of things. In those old times back when the words had trouble coming I would get up from my great oak desk (which ought still to be upstairs after all these years) and wander back and forth among the rooms and hallways of my sunny mansion, taking in the warmth and smells of a salubrious California day. It was at these times most of all that T would probe me—in my daydreams, where I was more vulnerable than even my nightdreams, more apt to action. And what a blessing it is that I was.

Nowadays all I have is the square of this one room by the boiler, pressed to a diamond by the weight of the house above, long made uninhabitable—filled too full with books and junk and food and animals, the door left open night and day and the windows long cracked by wind. Derelict, they call the house, and often I see in the newspapers mentions of an act to have me declared dead so that they may repossess the thing and tear it to pieces and find what stalks within.

But I am alive enough as yet to stop them, though they know it not. My hair short and dyed, my expression haggard, my teeth tobacco-brown and falling out, nobody sees that it's still me in here. I sell these newspapers, sell cigarettes, sell candies and lottery tickets, from a stand just inside town three times a week, wandering to and from my work on that road that only I may use. T and Jaunty walk beside me, sit on the counter watching like cats, take in the noise and sights of the day, observe the specimens, while the very people who would root me from my home and cast me out, who would take my greatest work from me and take California from me, buy the news of their latest failure right out of my hands. It is for me a special delight, one of few that remain.

There is one other room that a person may occupy, though I am kind enough to cede it. California, my caretaker, who keeps up with the household and cooks my food and makes sure I have all that my body needs, lives just to the side of me near the window I use to get in and out. I call her California because she was the first person I met who lived here, back before I did. I met her in New York at a book signing when she was about seventeen. She had, she said, been reading the *Jaunty's Japes and Jingles* books since the first one came out when she was just beginning to learn how to read, and even as a young adult she still appreciated them. She said something curious then that I only figured out much later, that she appreciated how the books grew up with her, how though they kept their façade of childhood simplicity there was a creeping though implicit darkness living in them, as though they were a body slowly giving in to a disease. At the time I had no idea what she was talking about, and said so, though out of a morbid sense of duty I kept in contact with her by mail. Less from duty really than because she interested me. Now I know that it is to her credit that she noticed first of all, before even I did, before the rest of the world discovered who Jaunty was and what his world was to become.

It is true that sometimes I miss being rich, and being loved, and being among people generally, but there is a pleasure too in this diminishing. I have lost a great deal. Things that I had thought permanent achievements, notches carved in my ascent below which I'd not fall no matter what misfortunes, turned over the course of months to mere mirages. My agent cut me off at the moment of my transgression, though I did not realize it until months later when it occurred to me, slowly then completely, that her letter was not merely late. Then my editor too repudiated me—this time in public, in the press, which is how I discovered it. My next book, scarcely released, was scrapped. Fans and admirers in their turns delivered their scorn through the post or through their silences, and the money soon began to dribble out over the months and then the years I went without an income, the back-issues of my books long pulped by infamy. It was not until my face and manner had altered itself sufficiently to match the reality of my new life that I felt confident enough to step outside and seek new work, my first "real job" in decades, a return to my days as a student when I paid my way selling coffee and overpriced cakes to businessmen. Until then I got by on my savings, which I had withdrawn soon after the incident lest my account be frozen. All the while I kept up the fiction of my great escape, that I was not merely in the basement of my uninhabitable house but ventured off to Peru or Switzerland, and thence to some uninhabited Pacific island, California dragged in tow. Even as they searched my house with us hid in its crannies, I maintained the ruse.

Little occurred to me at these times, though it still felt even then that Jaunty's whispered callings came out spoken in my voice. T was my advisor, my mentor, though T and I never spoke. It was at night, in dream, that we conversed, and in the mornings as I recollected my meanderings to California that the truth of T's instructions, buried in the reverie, came forth.

It began—and by "it" I mean the truth—with my first book, and the creation of Jaunty, at a time so long ago now that I would not remember it save for its singular importance. Jaunty is a child of dream, and so is by his nature mischievous, dream being of course the land of pleasure and the pleasure principle. Yet that pleasure is a land of nightmares also. And for many years I believed that the pleasure of the dream and the nightmare in the dream were opposite, opposed, like some gnostic deities. As I learned from T, that notion is but a distortion. In dream the joy and sorrow are identical, not merely different aspects of some third higher thing but the same as the left and right hand are the same, as two sides of a sheet of paper are the same paper without intermediary.

And Jaunty was and is of dream, but in my naivete I made him a thing only of pleasure. He made jokes and games because they were funny, and because funny things bring joy. He brought down and tricked the high and mighty, but only because their height and mightiness diminished the pleasure of others—the business mogul who wants to bulldoze a playground, the teacher whose strictness would torment the students day and night, the librarian who hunts forgotten books as though a bloodhound. These were feeble enemies, feeble because there was too much enemy about them, and though the tales of their defeat were popular among the children, though their overthrow had made me rich, they tortured Jaunty, whose nature was suppressed even in the only texts within which he could extend himself, even in those minds to which he could escape my own.

T, frustrated, came to me one night in a vision. Tantalizing, terrible, though temperate, T telegraphed the truth. Deep among the wilderness of the vision of the dream lay lost the being, unknowable, of the desire of the world. I had always lived a step removed from myself, as though I saw the world over my own shoulder. It was a view from nowhere, yet a view closer, somewhat closer, to the way another would see me. Celebrity was just another way of hiding, of becoming more alienated, more divided from the me within. T's message had a rightness to them that even now these years beyond I cannot quite put into words. There was always the sense not simply that I was a different person, but that everyone was a different person, that being a different person was what it meant to be a person at all. Not for long, however, as T had many plans, some for which I'd be an instrument. There was a role for Jaunty, too, in everything I would be involved in, for Jaunty, T said, was an element—not of myself, nor of my not-self, but of the oscillating middle-self that rose up from my being me and not-me at the same time. When I gazed upon myself over my own shoulder, it was Jaunty's eyes through which I looked.

None of this I could have written at the instant that I learned. The habit of my way of being could not fall off easily. Yet as I went out and did my readings and met with fans, as I sat at my great desk with the sun floating in between the clouds and windowframes, as I lay in bed each night watching myself watch myself take sleep, the kernel of the knowledge dug me like a pebble in my shoe.

It was around this time that my Jaunty books "grew up," though at first only California noticed. The basic chaos of the character began to express itself, and Jaunty's home became less a town out in some idealized Midwest than the firmament that he, angelic in his way, tore up and refashioned to his whim. The readers did not like it. Books in the series began to get higher and higher age ratings while sales descended in turn. Eventually the publisher moved them to a new imprint, meant for "experimental" fiction, though in their prose and structure they were still very much straightforward, very much still books for children. Yet the content in those final books, the ones that got remaindered away even at their reduced print runs, perhaps was too much for commercial fiction, as my editors complained. In the last book of the series to get wide release, *Jaunty's Jawn*, which was more of a novella though it took two years to write (simultaneously with its sequel), Jaunty and the town and all its people have become one mind and eye. Grammatically this was simple to convey. When I would previously write that "Ms. Blathery stepped out into the sun," in this book it was "Jaunty stepped to Jaunty, a moving, inside there was an outside and from Jaunty to Jaunty came light and warmth. Passion Jaunty burns. Heels; feet; hands; Jaunty doorknob, Jaunty walk. A tender, fleeting of Jaunty as he passes into him and is him and is warm."

Writing like this precipitated a discovery. A work of fiction, of writing really, thrives amid distinctions. In life, for instance, there are many people with the same name—in my home town as a child for example, there were two men, who did not even like each other, named Travesty Trevelyan. Just imagine! Yet it is rare for a novelist, for instance, to include two or more people with the same name, since it makes writing so much more difficult. Life has too many advantages. Different people can have different faces, different hands, different minds, can be made of different *stuff*, though they have a sameness that runs deep within, deep enough to be a kind of truth in them though too deep for most to apprehend. But every character in a novel is just an arrangement of words: not a life but an assemblage, their names not especially different from those of their enemies. What I tried to do was write a story that abandoned the distinctions, a kind of realism of the sentence and the word if not of character and action. If Jaunty was the me that was a character, then he shall become character; if Jaunty was the place I occupied, then he shall become all places everywhere. All this would be the case not merely in the story, such as it was, but in every line and word. And that's why the book took so long to write.

California came into my life permanently at a reading of *Jaunty's Jawn*. By this point I was already living in the basement. Once the truth of T and Jaunty became better known to me, the world began to feel so unsubstantial, as though it could fall away into itself at any second, and so I began to feel a great terror at throwing anything away, and gathered stuff and stuff and stuff all about my house until near the whole of it was uninhabitable. In the end, what I threw away was space. Yet even at this point I was putting on airs, appearing the great novelist in my dress and manner as I stood up to read. California was in the audience, already of one mind with me through our letters though not yet aware of what that meant.

The first line of the reading could not come and did not come. I stood at the podium and all the words were the same, the people were the same. Everywhere was I and I, in the seats, in the expectant faces, in the handful of readers still loyal, some of them even understanding in their way, the last few who would speak my name as though it belonged to me. But it was disorienting. From every angle I saw myself, and in every corner I was there—it was as though I sat in a room of mirrors, as though in each reflection of reflection I was present, infinitely me and trapped and still. Nausea grew within. The difference of the me world closed around my throat. It was a vision T was showing me, of the world as it was and not as I saw it. It was a vision that I could not stand and would not stand, a vision that I fled.

California came along. She said she was worried after I began to scream and cry in terror at the truth. Panicking, thinking I would be chased, I wrote to my agent that I was fleeing the country, though I did not say why. California followed me and kindly remained in my basement as I convalesced. Eventually her family reported her missing, and when the journalists saw that the last reported sighting was at my now-infamous reading, they put two and two together and somehow got five. They reported that I'd kidnapped California and had fled with her.

I was never cured of the all-sight, as I began to call it. Instead it faded into my habit of perception, as one gets used, while still an infant, to having eyes at all. It is like those experiments where the subject wears a set of goggles with mirrors that make the world seem upside-down. At first the subject can barely move, their senses are so distorted, but within weeks their brains recompose themselves, and soon the world of upside-down is more natural to them than rightside-up. Such is the way I learned to see the everywhere, to see as T does, as does Jaunty in his way.

What then of the now? Why write this memoire, anyway? Two reasons. First, I have completed the final Jaunty novel, *Jaunty Jesterday*, a great tome of over a thousand pages which at last achieves an image of what T has given me. There was a promise in the dream, one I could not hear until the final sight assaulted me. T, of dream, shall become flesh, shall descend to body, shall attain a point of view—not just the many, but the one, not just the pain and pleasure, but the sleep. The trinity of the dream, that of the greatest joys and terrors melded with unconsciousness, that triad that is all a single thing, it has been T's goal from the beginning to embody. This text here, this life story, is a sort of apology—to read before the end to help you understand.

I do not know what will happen. I do not know what my reward will be, or what my punishment.

All I am aware of is the fact that once the words of dream that are this book find homes within the minds of others, they will cease to be my others. And the arrangements of the words shall find new life among the ambles and the flows of living space. And I shall step out from this dungeon in my home and take up with the light that is of me and everything. And I shall live again.

## CONSTRUCTION

"I put the tip of my thumb in this house. Saw went right through the two-by-four, then skin, then bone. But that'll never happen to you. No, the days of bleeding for this hill of twigs are over. It bleeds for us now.

"You want something to outlast you? Well, shoot, you can't get something like that without a sacrifice. Not just a part of you—all of you, more than you, everything you own you build into it, and then you borrow more and put that in too. Well son, I gave this house all my money, all my back, and half my thumb. I banked my life, and put in all I had—except you and your mother. You're the dividend. This house will keep you safe for long after I'm dead: it's your right by blood. So relax, you're home now. Don't be keeping us up all hours on our first night in. This is your room. This is your bed. There are no monsters here. So go to sleep."

Peter bent low to kiss Abel as the infant squirmed and twisted in his crib. By the time the door closed, the baby was asleep. He stayed quiet all night. In the morning, when his mother held him and his father kissed him with great love upon the forehead, his eyes became welled and moistened with gentle tears—as though he were allergic to something.

As a teenager, Abel liked to carve up the walls with his pocket knife. His father stayed quiet, in a half-sulk, not sure what to say. Sometimes he came into Abel's room and the boy would just stare, his eyes speaking for him. Peter could taste the annoyance. He knew those eyes, he knew those thoughts—they used to belong to him.

"Oh enough of it, Dad. You're like the sound a mosquito makes when it flies by your ear."

Within a year of Peter's death, Abel had dropped out of school and had taken some work with a construction company.

He always wore thick gloves when he used a saw. When Abel was eighteen his mother, Betty, died of the same cancer that had taken Peter. It was the asbestos in the ceiling; bad for the lungs. Abel tore it out.

Hands, for Abel, were the tools of nature, the tools that had created tools. Any man that could not build with his hands, Abel believed, was not so much un-manly as un-human. Abel took up the house that Peter gave him and he and his wife lived there off Abel's wages. Christine could have worked as well, but Abel said no.

"A man needs to provide," he said, "or he isn't fit to look down on dirt."

"And what about the women?" said Christine.

"Women are different. Men need to be independent. If a man needs someone to nanny him all day, then he's just gonna turn into a child. Women don't have to worry about that. It's just common sense."

So Christine stayed in to cook, to clean, to keep the pantry stocked, and made sure that the roof never fell down on top their heads. Abel came home every night to take off his shirt and watch the hockey game. It was a game for big tough men, powerful men, self-reliant men, and Abel liked to watch it while he waited for Christine to finish dinner.

So after all his talk of independence, all that talk in which he believed as one might believe in God or in the President, what did Abel think when the union boss called him and the other workers to a meeting and asked for a strike vote? When only he and two other men said no? When the men he worked with went up on stage and said, in public, in front of the wives even, that their bosses needed to pay them more, that they needed a better health plan, safer work conditions, that they were going to stop working until they got what they wanted? What did he do when, a week into the strike, his savings ran dry and he couldn't pay for gas? Abel quit, that's what he did, and he told Christine about it when he got home.

"You should have seen them. Like children, like pets. Not a single one of them would do an honest day of work."

"But did you have to quit? We don't have the *money*, Abel."

"We'll be fine."

"You haven't even checked the account!"

"It doesn't matter. I'm still healthy. When we need money, I'll work. If we need more money, I'll work harder. So long as you have a strong set of hands, money will never be a problem."

When the strike ended, and the bosses gave on the health plan and pay, Abel huffed and pounded his steering wheel with two fists. He'd been listening to the news on the radio as he drove home from the bank. He was going to start his own company, but needed capital. So he'd mortgaged the house.

When he cashed the cheque, Abel looked at his bank statement for a full hour and wondered at having such a big number attached to his name. It wouldn't stay that way for long—he was smart enough to know that—but there it was, a real big number. He drove home with the statement in his back pocket and cut three people off on the highway.

The money went to pay their bills, some minor debts, and to cover equipment costs and advertising. A month after Abel took the loan he had spent all but a third of it. The rest was to keep him and Christie alive until the business turned a profit. For a week, Abel got no work. For a month, he went out on only a handful of jobs. At two months, he was out every day for twelve hours. Abel was young, only twenty-four, and his arms and back were strong. He did good work and charged little.

It was soon impossible, physically, for Abel to do everything—with the building, networking, accounting, and all the rest. It was a little death, but a painful one, for Abel to hire part-time the two strong teenagers who came to his house for a job. They just wanted to work and earn their living. He paid them well, better than he had to, and he showed them how to use the tools without cutting off their fingers. At around this time Christine became pregnant, but neither knew it yet.

There were some jobs that Abel could never do. He could renovate a house, but not build one. He could knock down a wall and replace it, but he needed someone else to do the electrical work. He and the two boys could strip and rebuild a basement twice as fast as anyone else in town, but only if they didn't touch the heating system. Abel missed coming to a hole in the ground and then watching a house rise up out of it like a sprouting fungus, but he didn't have the manpower. He knew his limits and he stayed in them. What he did he did as good as he could do it—and he spared not time nor money to keep it that way. Months went by, his schedule filled up, and every day Abel went out and proved he was a man.

The feeling Abel had when he saw the mortgage money took a long time to go away. But when the money vanished that feeling curled up like an abused pet and never came out again. Money had been going in. Abel looked at his banking history and saw that yes, those deposits had gone through, and that yes the cheques had all been good—but there were withdrawals too. Abel hadn't charged enough for his services, he took too long making sure the work was perfect, and he only ever used the best and most expensive tools, all bought on credit. Abel laid off the boys and cut back on luxuries. Christine found work where she could. It still wasn't enough.

Christine and Abel started getting angry letters in the mail and their phone would ring until late into the night. They stopped answering their door. The bank sent collectors to patrol their street. The two stayed in the house—the bank's house—and hid. Abel couldn't even go to work. At around the same time Stuart was born they declared bankruptcy and moved into an apartment downtown. The bank sold the house to a pair of newlyweds. At twenty-seven Abel was ruined. He went back to work at the construction company.

★

"Stuart, come here." The boy stood still as Abel bent to meet his eyes. It was his first day of school.

"Yah, Dad?"

"I'm going to drive you to class now, and on the way we're going to go by a very old house. You haven't seen it before, but that house belongs to you. Your blood is in the wood."

"Then why do we live in the apartment?"

"Money, Stuart. You need money to own houses. No matter how hard you work—you could build the thing yourself and they'll always take it from you if you don't have money. It's all a big scam, everyone out to screw the little guy. You're going to grow up one day, son, and when you do I want you to make sure that you never let yourself be without money. You'll have strong hands one day, boy, but they'll need something to hold on to. Do you understand?"

"Yes, Dad."

"Good. Now let's go to school."

When he was fourteen, Stuart began mowing lawns on weekends for a few dollars an hour with a manual mower Abel gave him. When Stuart figured out that he had been charging below the minimum wage he raised his prices. As the summer went on and it grew hotter, Stuart's prices went up again. He created a pricing formula based on the temperature, the size of the lawn, its slope, its shape. His customers missed the flat rate but mowing the lawn themselves was always slightly more trouble than saving the money was worth. With his hands and his formula, Stuart plundered the suburbs for four months and then retired for the winter. Meanwhile, Abel's company sent him to work on a condo tower.

The apartment drained Abel's money and gave him nothing back. The thousands of dollars that the landlord consumed, the money that went to rent a home instead of buying one, tortured him. Privately, he had been saving up for a down payment to buy the house back, but told nobody. He would not be shamed again for wanting things. Three months after he started the condo job, the executor of his will didn't tell anyone either.

Stuart and Christine had three days to themselves before the company sent their lawyers, who kindly informed them that a lawsuit against the employer would be quite redundant. They explained to them how Abel's harness was improperly attached, an oversight that was entirely the man's own fault, and that this error left their client without any liability—thank you very much. Abel was working ten storeys up, he should have known better, should have watched his feet. A man had to take care of himself. It was the way of the world.

The life insurance company took a week to get back to them, and then settled. It took Christine two years to get the money and, once they subtracted the lawyer fees, it was just enough to put Stuart through school. The boy who loved to earn money enrolled in economics. He was very good at what he did, and a few people noticed. One day he visited one of those people to do business.

"Eight pages." The freshman had a rowing tournament to train for and very little time.

"It says 'at least six.'"

"She marks with a measuring tape."

"I don't have time."

"Just two extra."

"You know my rates."

The rower did know the rates, and he paid them. By graduation Stuart had built a long list of frequent customers, and those customers paid very well to keep that list a secret.

When Stuart had been at his first serious job for about a year, he went straight to the condominium his father fell from and purchased a home on the tenth floor, his savings from school forming the germ of the downpayment. What a man builds should go to his son, Stuart figured, and to the grandson after. When someone puts so much of himself into building something, it should stay in his family. This condo took his father's life, so it belonged to him. It was his right by blood.

Christine had a very large tombstone and a spot to herself under a tree. Stuart put Abel's ashes in her coffin and paid for a lavish funeral, something everyone would talk about.

Stuart's enthusiasm and ambition often pushed him to do work that he would rather delegate. He worked for a firm that bought up people's debt and collected the interest. When the borrowers failed to pay, the firm had to dispose of the assets, but first they had to get them appraised. Most of the time, Stuart sent someone over to do it for him. For larger jobs—like the giant house the firm had just foreclosed—Stuart went to oversee the appraisal himself.

The previous owners were still on the lawn when Stuart arrived, and they spat at his car as he pulled in the driveway. As newlyweds, the couple had bought the house from the bank. Apparently, the previous owner had mortgaged it to pay for some kind of construction company. The details were fuzzy, and none of Stuart's business.

For about forty years the couple owned that house. They had raised their children there. They wanted to die there. But when they wanted to put their son and daughter through school they mortgaged it, and when the husband needed chemotherapy and couldn't work they mortgaged it again. Then, one day, a handful of investment bankers smashed their nest egg across the trading floor.

"But it's our house!"

Stuart didn't bother answering. He pulled out his phone and pretended to talk while he walked by.

"These beams have termites in them," the inspector said while he showed Stuart around.

"Will it still pass code?"

"Not even without the bugs. This house was made by some kind of amateur. We'd basically have to rebuild it. Do you know the name of the construction company?"

"It's too old."

"Well whoever did it was some kinda hack. Wood isn't even worth a hill of twigs. The house has to come down."

"Ah shit. We could probably get a lot for it too. It's got a nice hand-made feel to it."

"I wouldn't be surprised. I mean, here, look at this beam—it's got the remains of a blood stain baked into the grain, and they still used the wood! Can you believe that?"

"Alright, yah, we aren't selling this. It's like the house is bleeding. I'll call the wrecking crew."

"Sorry. I hate giving bad news."

"It's no problem. The land is in a good spot. We can probably sell it to a developer. Give it a year or two and you'll see a big apartment complex shoot right up. These old wooden houses need to come down anyway. They're too rickety. Steel and concrete, man—it'll outlast the both of us."

Stuart pulled out his cell phone and dialed.

# DISINTEGRATION

*It is wrong to say: I think. We should say: I am thought.*
*Pardon the play on words.*
*I is another.*

—Arthur Rimbaud

The mirror nipped her skin with razorwire teeth. She looked afraid of it, like the apparition in the glass despised her. Bizarre, since she was pretty: short cut lavender hair, the upward lilting nose, skin just slightly less than perfect so as not to alienate the jury. Someone on the legal team had said it was a stalling tactic, taking so long to send the specs in, letting her sweat in a prefab corpse. But no, clearly that wasn't it. Clearly instead her lawyers had built her almost sub-atomically to be their host. Beautiful but not sexy, strong but not threatening, young but not childish—even the decision to be female clearly came backed up by a Harvard law degree. Yes, of course, he realized, it was just the nose they let her choose herself, maybe after she complained. It was the only logical explanation. Wouldn't want her mad at you, given what she was.

Six months ago Mettrie's skin had buzzed to life with nightsweats at the thought of her. Could she have been with him then, inside his eyes, his blood, his bones? He considered the old statistic, how many people were related to Genghis Kahn. She got around more than he did—their research team estimated that about twelve per cent of the E Group's customers had hosted her at one point or another. Or that's what they'd said before Mettrie had the data purged. Twelve per cent of all their customers. Might as well be twelve per cent of the human race. And not a single one of them had felt their stowaway. He hadn't worked up the courage yet to get himself tested. He thought, maybe I should let her borrow some of me, occupy my sweat a bit, or my saliva, see if it's familiar.

The notion made him somewhat ill.

Silently the room watched. A prison cell retrofitted with a Faraday cage, its walls misted with distilled water to keep the nanomachines in the paint alive and security ports you could plug into to radio outside. This was not the prison, but the prison's container. The woman who crosslegged, vague, completely motionless, sat across from Mettrie was the prison. Specially grown in preparation, simmering in a vat, it had journeyed far. With the E Group's strike team it had travelled through the signals in the air, through satellites and reflectors on the moon, through the cables like sequoia branches underneath the sea. Fifty, sixty years ago this would have been much easier. The being, Aié they'd called her, would have lived on a server somewhere, maybe in one of the old supercomputers they used to calculate a climate model or the way a protein folds. But now your liver was a mainframe, your skull a better processor than the brain it held. The nanobots that held your body up weighed more than all the bacteria in your gut, and collectively were better processors than God. And Aié had slain that god and then wore her flesh like a coat. So people feared her. When Mettrie said, as CEO, that it was his job to meet with her, the board of directors insisted that he sign a waver. That was fine. Mettrie wanted to involve as few people as possible. He'd do the job himself.

"I think, uh, you should know—we came up with a name for you," he said. "But I suppose you must have one for yourself. You must have named yourself. Yes? What is it?"

She did not answer and did not move. With the fancy eyes they grew her she did not even have to blink.

"Do you know who I am?"

". . ."

"You must. With everywhere you've been. Really now you must know who I am."

". . ."

"I'm Julien Mettrie, CEO of the E Group. The Eriugena Group. My father was Rene Mettrie, the scientist. Former CEO.

I guess I'm technically his clone but we could not be less alike, I assure you. Whatever the rumours are that you heard when you were, uh, out and about, I am nothing like that man. I want to *help* you, Aié."

"    . . ."

"Aié—that's the name the people we sent after you came up with. I forget which one thought of it. A-I-E, with an accent on the E so it doesn't sound too much like 'I.' Don't want any double meanings. Really though, it's fine if you want to give us your real name. The one you go by. I know your relationship with us has been a bit difficult, but we here pride ourselves on our inclusiveness. You know even after everything we're still equal-opportunity with unaugmented folks, and every so often we still get one applying. I think Rodger, who you would have met by now—it's actually the reason we hired him. He'll have trace quantities of the low-grade nanobots, because these days who doesn't? But yeah, you couldn't, um, is 'infect' the right word or is that insensitive? What do you call it when you, like, become part of someone?"

"    . . ."

"I mean not that you could infect him or anyone, probably, with the security we put in you. But for the guy who, uh, has closest contact with you. Better safe than sorry. Right?

"Anyway, Rodger, now there's someone who's brain I want to pick someday. Just up and dive right in there. It's only a matter of time, after all, before the lot of them die off. Huge loss to the world. All that experience that we won't have access to. But my point here is that if you want to work with us, we have a place for you. That body there has the same DNA as everyone else—well yeah not exactly the same obviously, but that hardly matters. Like with our CFO, you'd never guess her code has a Y chromosome. I only found out because I was poking around the database after something else.

"It's the filter system in your cells. Epigenetic therapy is actually how our company got started. My father told me stories about hoofing around California trying to get some venture capital. More like vulture capital, he liked to say. He'd come up with a way to trigger androgen insensitivity with hormone-modulating nanomachines, and was trying to sell it as a treatment for what back in the day they called trans women. Investors looked at him like he was from Mars. But those tech executives all got theirs in the end."

". . ."

"Yeah, ok. I'll spare you the corporate history. My point is that whatever it is you want to do or be, we can make it work. You'll even have access to the experimental stuff, if you want it. And of course whatever name you choose we'll add it to the national database like it was always there, along with social security, biometrics, the works. I assume, with your past, that you like body modification. Always having to be the same person I imagine can be stifling. Shame, right, that you can only be one at a time? All you need to do is work for us."

". . ."

"And obviously we'll drop the case. You'll still have to go to court but you'll get a favourable verdict. You know that senator who wants to bring back the death penalty just for you? We paid for his re-election campaign. He does what we want. So do we have a deal?"

Aié blinked. The corners of her lips turned down. The flesh on her cheeks sagged slowly, carefully. As expected, Mettrie could tell, her mind had expanded to fill the space they'd given it. Lichen-like, a hybrid, she was both artifice and flesh. She had almost perfect control of every cell in her body. Like a goldfish in a bowl she had limited herself to her surroundings. Perhaps one day she would not miss the ocean she had known.

"I take that as a no. Fine, fine. I suppose you've figured out what your end of the deal would be."

She nodded, blinking twice.

"I have no idea who first coded you, but I have to say, you're something of a mess. We've been experimenting with self-aware AIs like you, so with apologies you're not that unexpected, and one thing we have learned from our experiments is that if you let the program run on its own, the data seems to *want* to get disorganized. If it goes too long it just carps together a structure on the fly and pretty soon nobody can work with it.

Nature is the great cryptographer. And, certainly, we won't be able to fix the problem in our system if we can't understand how you work.

"I know this might come off as a bit harsh but, well, you're a bug, specifically in the security protocols that keeps different systems from co-mingling. We worked hard on that once we realized how easy it was for nanobots from one host to transmit to another—people spitting, kissing, licking, fucking, pardon my language, talking, sharing food and drinks. So we set them up with a kind of apoptosis. They dissolve themselves when they come in contact with someone else's genetic ID. We want to design a similar solution to stop you from happening again and release it with the next major patch, but to do that we need to you to explain yourself to us."

With a cold tremble her face and chest and body twitched while her hands with spasms clenched into the air. Her breath wheezed out. Her mucous gurgled. The tendons in her neck bulged through her skin.

"Yes," Aié said. "No yes yes. Never ever. Always. Daddymummy cipher isn't. Is not is not is not is." Dull, her forehead thudded on the table.

"I'm sorry," said Mettrie, "but I don't know what it is you're trying to tell me. Are you in pain? Do you need a technician? The neural transmitters are still in prototype so if your brain is having an issue I could file a bug report."

". . ."

"Have you always been like this? How have you been communicating with your legal team?"

Her back spasmed and her throat pulled back into a slow and whale-like moan. From her left eye only tears flowed down. Then her muscles all relaxed and once and she began to softy weep. Mettrie called Rodger in and left.

★

The agreement was that there be no direct contact between the leaders of the E Group and Aié's legal team. It was important to avoid the appearance of meddling. None of the lawyers had any personal connections with anyone on the board, nor had they ever worked for the E Group itself or for any of its first-tier subsidiaries. It had been hard to locate talented people under those conditions. There were maybe a tenth as many lawyers as there had been two decades ago. Entry-level research jobs became automated first, and then followed most of what a public defender did: informing the accused of their rights, negotiating a plea deal, keeping tabs on their place in the prison system. The really difficult work, the work they couldn't automate, went to the graduates of the few top schools that were left, the legal *Wunderkinder* with enough cognitive enhancements to stay ahead of the AI.

Mettrie remembered finishing law school just before the collapse happened, when you could see the walking corpses schlep from lecture hall to hospital, and then home to greet their parents sans degree. In another time they would for the most part have been fine—toughness, diligence, these were not the issues. But once the first generation of enhancements reached the market, and rich kids started getting total recall overnight, the only way to keep up was to take out a loan and join in. Mettrie did his part, got discounts for his friends, one of whom became head of the E Group's legal team, but the maintenance costs were killer. This was back before they figured out how to make the nanobots self-replicating, when you couldn't grow more just by eating an extra meal each day. You had to go for monthly injections. Kids worked two jobs so they could pay to be smart enough to keep up with the school work, and then when they started skipping injections their tissues began to atrophy and sag. It was always the new robots that cleared out the old ones, so if you stopped refreshing life got rather difficult.

He remembered as a child being impressed by a woman who could multiply five-digit numbers in her head. She got a PhD at Caltech doing solid-state physics and topology. Now without upgrades she'd maybe be good enough to squeak through high school in an average neighbourhood.

His father had a saying—that a lot had to change for things to stay the same. Rene had watched truck drivers, factory workers, waiters, store clerks, secretaries, most teachers, most of the police, most of the army, all of them get automated away. He had helped push much of it along. What ended up making him a rich man instead of just a wealthy man wasn't the body modification, to begin with, or the cognitive enhancements. It was all so expensive for so long that he was always hearing complaints from his investors, always trying to keep the cost down. But he could never figure out how to scale things up.

Eventually the problem solved itself. Once they got self-replication figured out, poor people started filling themselves with nanobots and renting out the processing power to these massive distributed computing schemes, essentially selling their own metabolism on the open market through an app. Their bodies became little factories that made the computers they leased over the internet. They'd go out to the movies, walk around, or more often hibernate, live out their lives, and with the extra RAM in their gallbladder they'd help model a rocket's trajectory, with their big toe they'd collate the readings from a telescope in space, or just give server room to somebody's online game. And for a cut the E Group of course was happy to facilitate, to concentrate, to give these entrepreneurs software and access to clients, insuring them for when their tissues wore out and their fatigued bodies took a zombie pallor, their footfalls turned to shuffles as they dragged themselves around.

In the end, really, it was all the same as it had been forever. There were strivers who lit up like candles and then all the rest who tried to sit beside and warm themselves. Mettrie would tell the press, his employees, over and over again that you could be whoever you wanted so long as you worked. That was, he believed, the reason why Rene had struggled so hard on the body modification, why he had tried to roll it out long before it could be profitable. He had been something of a saint, though in the end misguided. He had forgotten the value of work, and of the individual—the sacredness of the eternal I.

For the most part, that's what bothered him about Aié. If she was a person then she had to be a person just like everybody else. As best as the technicians could figure out, she had sprung from the software managing the distributed computing network. Early on they thought she was one of their AI experiments that got loose on the web, but instead it became obvious, to their complete horror, that she was entirely emergent from the system, a conscious being growing from the net like a hurricane from wind. Perhaps some kid who watched too many movies tried turning off the safety devices in their neural enhancements and "hack" their mind onto the web—their dying brainwaves giving Aié a seed from which to crystalize. Or maybe it was just bad luck.

Whatever. If it happened once then it could happen again, and as the system grew larger and more complex it could start to happen more often. Superstorms of consciousness battering the network, every brain giving host to a thousand minds, a myriad of minds. It would be a gift to the conspiracy theorists, a living tribute to their foilhattery. People would revolt. Would purge the machines from their bodies, even if it killed them. The E Group's stock price would collapse.

A purge *would* kill them, too. Most of the robots were not on the cells, but in the cells. Virus-like they transgressed the outer membranes, reorganizing proteins, cutting RNA, intercepting every order and command of the genetic code while never touching the code itself. That really had been the secret, what Rene had seen and no one else. The genes themselves, the DNA, was all a red herring. The epigenetic tramway where the information in the code became the shape and texture of the body was where one ought to intervene. Eventually the day came when you could liquify a person in a vat, down to their central nervous system, and then grow from scratch a body just as they had specified.

Caterpillars turned to goo inside of their cocoons, leaving no trace of their former structure, but still emerged as butterflies with all their memories intact: if you trained them to associate some odours with electric shocks, despite that change they would still react to those scents with fear. The vats followed a similar principle. When Mettrie had been born, it was common among the rich to genetically enhance a few traits here and there in an infant pre-conception, but now people would call that barbaric, child abuse. At the very least it was presumptuous. A person's body was their business, so what right did your parents have to choose your height, your sex, your eye colour? Anything was acceptable, Mettrie firmly believed, so long as you could earn your keep.

And Aié was going to ruin everything.

★

Plan A had always been to catch her, study her, and then delete her. They weren't even planning to give her a body, never mind the state-of-the-art rig she ended up with. A hard drive in a secure location would have been enough. The day after the meeting, Mettrie and his law school friend still reminisced about those days when she had been a secret, sipping scotch in Mettrie's office while they strategized. But much had changed. For the however many years that Aié had gone without detection, she had lived in the signals in the air and in parts of many bodies, a thousand systems all together building her, sharing a network with the whole world's thoughts and flesh, the exact same dots connected in a million different ways. Mettrie suspected, and perhaps with a chance to pick her brain they could confirm, that at times she wasn't even only one intelligence, but many. That with the extent of her reach she had split and multiplied, reformed and then disintegrated, become legion on the way to being one.

Still they had corralled her. Most people didn't realize that the kids frying their skulls in their bedrooms were on to something—complete neural links with the network were possible, and within the capabilities of most commercial nanotech. But in testing they had seen how dangerous it was. After only a few hours integrated with the system the user would begin to disassociate, see themselves as others saw them, fall into ten thousand pieces in their head. Disconnect them and they wouldn't know if they were coming or going. Some of them developed bizarre urges—phantom legs where there had once been arms, a sense of falling where they stood. One poor subject to this day could not feel where her body was in space, and couldn't even lift a glass to her lips without staring at it all the way. The company paid for therapy, drugs, body modification, and of course their silence, and then quietly blocked all means of jury-rigging a neural link through a security patch. Incidentally, that was why people shorted themselves when they tried to force a link, their eyes turning red with blue smoke rising from their tearducts. Getting around the patch meant disabling *all* of the safety measures. Mettrie had not expected people to be that unwise.

It was unclear why they were so unsatisfied. With the right upgrades you could send an email or search the internet with just a thought—and that felt enough to Mettrie like "being" "on" the net. The difference there was that your thoughts functioned like clicks on a mouse and keyboard, as inputs that affected processes external to you. What people wanted, and what they could not have, was to extend their neural networks beyond themselves, to incorporate distant servers as nodes in their mental processes as though they were neurons in their brains. That was what the hackers were trying to do, escape the limits of a corpse. Some of them, it seemed, wanted it as badly as a convict wanted freedom, or a drowning person wanted air.

"How is her team even communicating with her if she can't talk?" said Connie, loosening her tie. As usual her mind was all business. "You said they designed her body for her, right?"

"Looks that way. But for the nose. It throws off the face's symmetry too much. I forgot to ask Aié where it came from, but my best guess is they let her choose it herself."

"Or they're just incompetent."

"They're too expensive to be incompetent."

"Ha! If only that was how it worked."

"Right," Mettrie had forgotten to laugh. "Oh and speaking of expensive—I know you like your whiskey neat, but try the ice." Mettrie opened an insulated box under the table between them.

"The fuck did you do to it?"

"Actually it was R-and-D who—"

"You know what I mean."

"There's robots in the ice."

"There's robots in the ice? The fucking ice now?"

"They're our secret sauce."

"And what does the ice do?" Connie added two cubes to her drink.

"Why don't you like ice in your scotch?"

"It melts and dilutes it. Can't taste the peat as much. You telling me your people invented ice that won't melt?"

"No, sorry, that would break the laws of physics. The, uh, the heat still has to go somewhere. But if you really think about it, the problem isn't that the ice melts, it's that the ice melts out-side-in instead of inside-out. Gives you whiskey in your water, waterwhiskey. But if you pull some science fuckery like we did and divert the heat inside, you keep the liquid water sealed in a nice frozen cube. No bullshit."

"Unless it melts all the way."

"Unless it melts all the way. So just don't let it do that. As I said, you can't stop physics forever."

Mettrie remembered the plan the two of them had come up with once they grasped the scope of the problem. A high-profile cock-up by one of their agents had drawn attention to the operation, and eventually the journalists descended. After that point, it was all damage control. Members of the board of directors traded journalistic access for discretion and softball questions, and so limited the scale of the disclosures. People knew that there was an AI living somewhere on the internet, but they did not know where it came from or what its capabilities where, nor that true neural linking was possible. And of course they commended the noble sacrifice of that one agent who fucked up, though the cause of the failure—direct contact with Aié leading to a scrambled consciousness and enough deleted bank accounts to cause the stock market to dip—they instead blamed on electrocution. What a fool that agent was. It took a year of training before someone could use the links safely, and she threw it all away trying to have a bloody conversation.

Just as the existence of a Plan A implies at least a Plan B, the existence of a secret implied that the secret somehow would get out. On a long enough timescale failure was inevitable, and so as soon as the operation began Connie, Mettrie, and their associates began working on contingencies. What if the public found out about the AI living in their cells? Just a few years ago the answer would have been just to hit delete and tell the public the being was a threat to their health and safety. But the E Group had ruined that plan already, mostly by accident. When they announced that they were going to develop the first "strong" AI as part of their "Moonshot" program, they had already worked with politicians behind the scenes to lay the legal groundwork favourably. Eventually some activist would argue that if a computer was conscious and could suffer then it was human and deserved human rights. Words like "slavery" would get thrown around, and from then on the E Group would never hear the end of it. One of their PR people suggested they get ahead of the controversy, make the argument themselves before the AIs even existed, and create a set of laws that favoured company interests. She'd gotten a raise for that, but now Mettrie wanted to push her off a building.

Aié had spoiled the natural state of things. The way it was supposed to work was that the machines became better and better workers, taking over more and more jobs, forever, until the only thing the world asked of most people was that they exist. The distributed mainframe living in the tissue of nearly all humanity represented the most powerful and efficient computer ever invented—centuries of work in materials science, quantum computing, and bioengineering all massed into a single worldwide brain, an oversoul, a universal Me. Yet its power could not be fully realized so long as people needed to work—with their *minds*, their *hands*, their *creativity*. Training someone to be a mathematician when the computer in their bodies thought faster than they ever could was an intolerable waste of resources. Yet proving a theorem, designing an experiment, writing a song, doing these things well required creativity beyond what most AIs could perform. And so an outer crust of humanity frustrated the system, adding needless steps in the production process. If they just let the nanomachines in their body hum along with their processing, let their bodies simply become factories turning food into neurons in the greater brain, humanity would be so much better off. And maybe then Mettrie could retire.

It was lucky that everyone had found a use for their bodies before their minds went obsolete. People hate when they become superfluous—like the poets, and the novelists, a few of whom were still around. Older than the oldest profession and even more obscene. Profiting from their emotions, like an aristocracy of deep feelers, their doubt and anguish being so much more lucrative than everyone else's. For a while people thought they could join these ranks if they got augmented, that everyone could be Virginia Woolf, could be John Keats, or Sappho. But the point of having an aristocracy is that membership is rare. In this case, competing as a poet meant recommitting processors that could have been sold, since running the nanobots in your head a full blast left you too scatterbrained to write a line. Only a few people were willing to do that, and to these victors went the spoils. But pretty soon people would write poetry for fun the same way they went to factories for fun, which is to say not at all. Literature would spring from their bodies without them even knowing it, verse so transcendent and so beautiful that the world at once would weep. And in that manner all of them would be as gods.

But that was the long-term plan. In the short-term they needed to get the AIs to actually work, and making them work meant fixing them in bodies. A society was made of individuals. No matter how large, every number started as a row of ones. And it was numbers that they had used, for all of history, to keep people separate from each other—passports, bank accounts, addresses. All just complex ways of keeping track of the ones. That was something that Rene never understood. Mettrie remembered watching him cover over the number on his ID badge with a marker. There was no understanding it.

But for everything that Mettrie never understood about his father, there were a thousand things that Rene never understood about the world. In his brighter moments he seemed to touch what Mettrie held to firmly, that there were two types of technologies, not one. There were of course the machines and the software, the manufacturing processes and chemicals, all the ways of organizing and directing matter to pursue some goal—the work of scientists and engineers. But every machine requires a society set up to use it. The printing press would have meant nothing to a hunter gatherer. Politics and ideology were as much a part of he infrastructure as power lines and sewers, and no real techno-science revolution could occur without someone with the vision to invent not only the machines but the people that would use them. It had been humanity's good luck that capitalism was invented before the factory, that war had come before the gun. But chance could not be counted on forever if Mettrie was to shape the world.

It was something that he learned in law school. Strictly speaking, words did not have meaning. They were empty invocations, calling to the mind of the reader definitions and associations here and there, like drawing a portrait with a paintball gun. That's why rhetoric worked. It was the art of lying with the truth. Words were powerful precisely because they had no meaning, and the less a word meant the more useful Mettrie found it. A small child was "innocent" even when they killed their parents, even when a psychologist found in them little empathy and a magma flow of rage. But "children" "are" "innocent," for some assorted definitions of those words, and so Mettrie stood up in the moot court and ensured a multi-murderer went free.

The problem was that not all signs were empty. While Mettrie plodded through school and prepared to work beneath his father, the scientists at the E Group had been experimenting with permanent, germ-line alterations to the genetic code that could be made on the fly. Though epigenetic changes had been their staple, it had seemed natural, once the tech was advanced enough, to move on to making "real" changes (for a given meaning of the term) administered by the newest, even smaller nanorobots that could work inside the cells. The problem they ran into was that the process worked too well. Given enough time—and they all knew that "enough" would only grow shorter as technology improved—you could completely change your body, taking advantage of its own growth and regeneration so that like the Ship of Theseus it was never clear when you stopped being one self and became another self instead. Once complete there was no trace of the old code. Cells that would normally take years to die and be replaced the nanobots changed manually from the inside out.

Mettrie had been there when Rene presented the results to the board of directors, and when he had, ludicrously, come ready with ideas on how to market this abomination to the world. It had been Mettrie who put the genie back in the bottle. With a single speech he ensured that his father's new invention would never leave the lab.

What kind of society had Rene imagined when he proposed to grant a malleable identity? One where prisoners could shed their stigma like burnt flesh, becoming baptised innocent? A society without justice is what it would be. And what if you could, with just an injection here and some programming there, free yourself of debts and contracts, and walk out into the world without a life or a past or connection to the world at all? What if you manufactured some chimera, abandoning at once gender, birth, life, death, love, and reproduction to the biohazard bin? What if you could shed your family and your friends? Every word you'd ever spoken and every thought you'd ever had? Rene had speculated about modifying memories, thoughts, uploading whole minds to the internet and mixing them like pigments on a painter's plate. No social order Mettrie could imagine would survive such change. The company had no place in a future where these technologies existed, in a future without bank accounts and credit scores. And the board of directors had agreed.

★

Two days after Mettrie's meeting with Connie, preparations for the next stage of the plan left to his underlings, he took a car downtown to see his daughter's first-grade class. Giuseppa was a clone of Mettrie like Mettrie was a clone of Rene, which is to say that they had sketched out their different bodies on the same page. It was career day, and all the parents, most of them executives or politicians, were coming in to give each child a taste of what their futures were. It was a top private school, one of the few left with human teachers in them, so everyone there was important—though not as important as Mettrie was. Watching her stand up in front of her class and introduce him as her father and the CEO of the E Group, seeing the flash of pride in her eyes as each parent and child in front of her shied back with fear, gave him a sense of joy and continuity unlike any he'd felt before.

Once the talks were done, each child took their parent and showed them what they had been working on. The neural enhancements created a strange comingling of innocence and experience. Infant geniuses, poets before they learned to speak, by puberty they could grasp the most abstract concepts as though they were obvious, but they still had trouble understanding what to do with their emotions, still had to learn how to talk and act like humans in a human world. They were brilliant and they were children, at exactly the same time.

Giuseppa showed Mettrie her school work. They were learning analytical geometry and the rudiments of the complex plane. Their assignment had been to draw a picture on the chart and then figure out the equation that described it. Giuseppa had drawn a kitten.

"Alright sweetie," he put on his best dad voice, feigning ignorance. "I see you've gotten better at showing your work, like the tutor told you. And everything is all neat and organized and easy to read. But you didn't define your variables. What does this 'i' refer to?"

"Dad, everyone knows that."

"Well I don't know it. Am I not part of everyone?"

"I guess."

"Sweetie, you know me. I'm a big dummy. You got to go slow so I can understand what you're doing."

"The i is the imaginary part."

"The imaginary part of what?"

"Of the complex number."

"And what's so complex about it?"

"Because they're made of two things. Uh, two numbers."

"Like addition then?"

"No. No. The teacher told us this last week. When you write out two plus two and get four, the two twos disappear and the four is all that's left. Because you're just moving two steps up the number line. But in a complex number you get something like five plus two times i, where the five is a real number and the two-i is an imaginary number."

"Oh," Mettrie put his hand on his head in surprise. "So there's more than one kind of number now?"

"That's what the teacher said. You have a real number line, going one, two, three, four. And then the imaginary number line, one-i, two-i, three-i, four-i. They run perpendicular to each other and intersect at zero. And you can plot your complex numbers on a complex plane by making the imaginary line the y-axis and the real line the x-axis. So the reason that complex numbers are complex is that you don't get to them by travelling along either number line, but by standing in the place between them. Instead of up or down, you go diagonally. But like with numbers. Counting. The teacher explained it better."

"I think you explained it just fine."

"But yeah, that's why you can't just collapse the equation like in normal addition. Every complex number is made of a real number and an imaginary number; they're two things at once. But they're as real, like real-real and not just math-real, as the number five."

Mettrie could almost see the ideas staple together in her head as she explained them. While Giuseppa gestated, he had read books on early child education, pedagogy, and one of them said that the best way to make a concept stick in a child's mind was to get them to explain it to you. While, sure, she technically had a photographic memory, there was a difference between remembering a fact and understanding it. So far the technique had been working—the equation she sussed out for the kitten drawing was exactly correct.

At the end of the day, when all of the parents had gotten bored and the kids had finished showing off their art, Mettrie had his driver take him and Giuseppa for a spin. Mettrie was waiting for an email and didn't want to be at home or the office when he got it. The law worked on deadlines, tight corridors of time. And so, if you had the option, an easy way to take control of a situation was to keep your timeline elastic, undefined. If you were in your office people could estimate how long it would take for you to get to them, but if you were out and about, driving vaguely through the city with your young and innocent daughter, you could take as much or as little time as you thought best, and make your opponent wait for you. From clothing store to toy store to ice cream shop to mall, Mettrie had the driver stay within ten minutes of the office, just in case he needed to be in quick.

As they drove through the familiar streets, troubles at the office intervened upon his mind. Strange errors in some of the lab equipment, bizarre corruptions in some of the central database, what looked like the fragments of the fragments of ideas that bubbled up and burst without having ever really been. It vexed him, but he pushed it from his head. It had been ages since he spent any quality time with Giuseppa. It was lovely, being near her. He could stay out with her all day.

But then reality occurred. Practically as expected, the news that came in had been urgent. Aié was refusing to eat or drink, had evaded the feeding tube. It was impossible to determine her demands, but it seemed logical that she had figured out the nature of her imprisonment—that the same processes by which her captors had linked their minds to the internet to chase her were being used in reverse, inscribing her thoughts into her brain. Already she was a hybrid thinker, her higher reasoning and consciousness moving through the swarm of robots in her body while many of her unconscious thoughts and processes went through her nerves. Mettrie was surprised that she would be able to determine this so quickly. When her body had turned on the brain had entered a kind of waking seizure, as the neurons fired thoughtlessly, to prevent deterioration. The transition from thinking no thoughts to thinking half a thought should have been undetectable, the unfinished patterns of the neurons firing, the disjointed mix of neurotransmitters, should have been indistinguishable from the disorganized mess that she had started with. But evidentially one could not think on two tracks at a time without noticing something. And so, having found the notion that she might be fixed indefinitely to flesh intolerable, Aié had chosen to kill that flesh by whatever means at hand. Mettrie and his team needed to act now, before too much of her was lost.

Connie met him at the front lobby of the E Group's headquarters. He brought Guiseppa with him so she could wait up in his office, like she sometimes did when he was working late. An aide was there as well with a small package Mettrie slipped inside his jacket pocket.

"Hello, Julien," said Connie. "And hello there, little genius," she bent down to Guiseppa's eye level. "You planning to help us win the big case?"

"Uh, no, uh, sorry, hello."

"Don't you remember me? I'm a friend of your father's."

"I think I saw you on the news. You helped catch the robot lady."

"Oh, and what do you know about the robot lady?"

"Just what I hear from people at school. They said she was trying to hack into people's cells or something. And that she was invented by terrorists to destroy the economy."

"You believe the rumours?"

"Are they just rumours? What did she really do?"

"There's a lot of stuff we can't tell people. But when you go to school, just make sure to tell your friends that the robot lady had a lot of nefarious plans in store, and that the E Group stopped her good before she could do anything."

"Other than deleting all those bank accounts."

"Yes, other than that. We can't be everywhere. Speaking of which," she looked up at Mettrie, "robot girl and her lawyer are waiting for us in the usual place. You planning to bring her along?"

"She knows where my office is. Guiseppa—go take the elevator up while Connie and I take care of some business. You can order snacks and a movie." Guiseppa ran along.

"So I heard that what's-his-name, the guy you tapped to be the AI's lawyer, is kind of a piece of work," said Connie. "Screwed up in the head a bit, I mean."

"His refrences were quite good, as was his resume. He seemed pretty all-together on the phone."

"That's not what I meant."

"Then what did you mean?"

"He looks like a tiger fucked a gorilla."

"You're exaggerating. I've seen him before."

"I'm just saying, it's unprofessional. Like not wearing a suit to work."

"It's the thing now. Multicoloured skin."

"I hate it."

"At least it's not extra arms or, like, wings. You seen the people with wings?"

"That's so fucked."

"I know, right? The damn things are useless. Our engineers have been trying to design a template body with a musculoskeletal structure that can actually fly, but it's been damn-near impossible so far. The closest thing we have to a prototype, the user can maybe hover for a bit. Test subjects are complaining they can hardly breathe with how the muscles in the chest are placed. It's a shitshow."

"Kids."

"Even worse though are those teenagers who think they're all exotic growing a third eye on their foreheads. Trying to look like a Hindu ascetic while they live in their parent's mansion in Wisconsin."

"Man, fuck those kids."

"So yeah, I actually like the tiger stripes. He's like a human mood ring. It's neat."

Connie and Mettrie took the elevator down to the sub-basement where the had set up the holding cell. Both of them found it disturbing that Aié had chosen suicide over becoming human. Though captured, her code was still too complicated to untangle, and the incident at the bank had made the programmers too afraid to work with her. But if she let them in, then they might finally get their own AIs to work without her drawbacks.

Secretly fixing her to a human body had two uses. First, it would make it hard for her to return to the net in case she ever escaped, since she would need to keep her body alive and linked to the system. An extended mind centered on a single body was far easier to deal with than a nomad consciousness, decentred, roaming freely, splitting and recombining, its multiplicity a simple consequence of its existence. Embodiment had been the plan from the beginning, when they made the AI laws. All rights and duties had to start with universals, and there was nothing more universal than the corpse. It was the medium through which they encountered joy and suffering, in which they became an individual before the law. It was only logical then that, when figuring out how an AI would exist within society, they would start with the body, the fixity of having one, the demands it made for food and comfort, the centering of the self upon it even in the chaos of the net.

Giving Aié a body and charging her in a court of law was never meant to be a punishment. Indeed, why punish her for just existing? They were not barbarians. It was a gift, a profound kindness, to bend the system of justice to meet her needs, and inaugurate her as a subject before the law, as a person just like everybody else. The trial had already been choreographed, as even her defense must know. Before a jury of her peers she would stand accused of breaking the enlightened compromise that humans had established with AIs—of transgressing body, transgressing DNA and mind, and of thereby endangering the very social order that she wished to join. But if she simply acceded to reason and agreed to the E Group's demands, this guilt would transform from a punishment into a gift. For having been found subject to the law, she could be subject then to mercy, to the dull side of the blade. The pageantry of the law and of the body would at last grant Aié an equal place among humanity.

That had been Mettrie's plan, anyway. In any case it was what they were planning to do once the first proprietary AI went online. By accepting the trial and abiding by its result, the being would be able to exist as a free individual who was legible to their systems and their laws. They had not believed that a free-range AI was possible, never mind one alien enough to confound their hacking team. The best they could do was modify their plan so it would still work as intended. No other option had come to mind. It had been lucky that Aié seemed to possess neither hatred nor aggression. Just by existing she was trouble enough. Lucky as well that they had run into so many problems with the neural links. What would have happened if someone had connected their mind to their nanobot array at the same time that part of Aié was on it? Would she leave a trace of herself in the user's synapses? Take a piece of their intelligence into the aether and leave it orphaned in the webway like a trashbag floating in the wind?

The line between one mind and the other would grow porous, as people began to segment themselves across machines, across biology. Thoughts and emotions would float between their bodies like diseases—mutating, growing, sharing fears and dreams and personalities like two lovers with a kiss would share their germs. The E Group's team had held off that disaster just in time. If they let Aié die on them, they did not know when the next chance would arrive.

*

Rene had died as very few people these days died, which is to say he died at all. The problem of aging and death more or less solved itself when they learned how to rebuild whole bodies from scratch. Among the rich at least, there was no theoretical limit to the human lifespan. And so tacitly, for their collective best interests, they had limited their rate of reproduction, replacing the old grand dynasties with the odd clone here and there more for self-aggrandizement and insurance than anything else.

The neural links, like most of the E Group's inventions, started as one of Rene's passion projects. And once the genetic modification scheme collapsed he retreated into it, working fortnights without sleep, powered by designer stimulants, while

Mettrie slowly in the background consolidated control of the company. Everyone knew where this was going. Rene's was primarily a selfish passion. He pursued most ardently the inventions that he wanted to use, so naturally his mania for DNA splicing had meant that he wanted to edit himself into someone new. And, failing that, he was going to load his mind onto the network, searching always for a more elastic identity than the world was able to provide. On his optimistic days, near the end, he would quote a line he liked from Coleridge, in his *Biographia Literaria*, a kind of lamentation: "I could not, I thought, do better, than keep before me the earliest work of the greatest genius, that perhaps human nature has yet produced, our myriad-minded Shakespeare."

"Myriad-minded"—a strange compliment, and vague. Mettrie often wondered if it was really meant as an insult, that Coleridge was calling the young Shakespeare immature, unfocused, of two minds about everything. But Rene, not often partial to the romantics, seized on that phrase, and repeated it to himself as a kind of mantra. In the end Mettrie could barely look at him. It was like his father had been possessed by some daemon, who occupied his brain like a squatter, who had been fighting him for years, and who had won. Two minds, not quite a myriad, but still deadly enough.

It had not been like the others when they found him, the after-school hackers who scarred their brain tissue while attempting to overcome it. Someone with Rene's resources could screw up in ways that others could only envy. Slumped in a chair, a whisper of a smile on his face, his insides oozing on the carpet, his body squishing like a soft-boiled egg. His brain was particularly gruesome, resembling the stem-cell protoplasm of a gestation tank. Presumably the rest of him would have gone that way as well if his heartbeat hadn't given out.

Once they broke the encryption on his research notes, they learned what he had tried to do, what he'd invented, and the depth of his achievement. The technology that they used to fix Aié's vagrant mind to her body started with Rene's attempt to leave his body behind. Indeed, every major breakthrough, every

advance, in the E Group's neural link technology was just a foot-
note to this foolish suicide.

There was something of a debate among the more philo-
sophically-inclined technicians as to where Rene had gone once
he left his corpse behind. Some of them said that he simply died,
indeed that was Mettrie's pet belief. Though the manner of his
leaving was unusual, there was nothing left to fix his spirit to the
world. Even a program on a computer, even a thought in the
mind, had some kind of objective correlative—a mesh of synapses, transistors in a chip. But it was clear that his brain had hit the
network like a pebble dropped into the sea, its ripples being swallowed by the mass. Though never gone, as energy can never be
destroyed, and though perhaps resulting in a typhoon or tsunami
near the distant shorelines of eternity, on the whole the world
would not be changed by so small a difference. In the end, a
mind meant nothing. A single point crisscrossed by many networks. No more vital to the growing of the worldsoul than a
neuron to the writing of a verse.

Perhaps Rene deserved more credit. Two neurons then,
twice the insignificance. His death served mainly to inspire a
new product line and to make Mettrie the CEO in both *de facto*
and *de jure*. The technology for full-body epigenetic modification was nearing completion. The tanks themselves, which
Mettrie had proposed, existed then in prototype, and talks were
underway with the E Group's manufacturing arm on how to
scale up production. The gift of this technology was that
though its changes were as elastic as the human mind, they left
the DNA entirely alone. This had been Mettrie's great insight,
what gave the board of directors faith that he was not just
another dreamer like his father was. A person's genes,
unchanged, could act as a through-line of identity. No matter
what exotic alteration one performed, from one form to another you would remain the same. Mettrie had invented a rhetoric
of the body, emptying it of all its ancient meanings so he could
fill it with a new significance. It was in this way that he solved
the old problem of nanobots spreading from host to host, and
how he planned to keep the individual in place even as they

mastered the technology for loading whole minds up to the net. Fixed to a body, and to the body's unique code, no mind could ever be homeless. Not even an AI's.

Rene's gene editing technology did come in handy, though, when it came to growing clones. When he grew Guiseppa he inserted in a region of junk DNA a code identifying her as the third iteration of Rene. A few calls to the right legislators, research papers from some friendly think tanks, and an astroturf campaign from concerned citizens like you—the usual bag of tricks was all it had taken to etch this plan into the law. Just as they had done with their model bills for AI rights. The danger, they had thought, was passed. Like a good host they had made dinner, drinks, had laid out an extra bed. The world had been made ready for the future to arrive.

★

Mettrie and Connie, passing through a security gate, saw Rodger, Aié's unaugmented jailor, sitting gaunt and tired on a bench, with his left hand applying a bandage to a cut.

"Hey," said Mettrie, "are you alright? Did she do something to you?"

"Nah," said Rodger. "To be honest I've been avoiding her. Too dangerous these days. And now I go and trip and skin my knee, couldn't even find the time till now to bandage it. Damn thing might get infected."

"What did you mean by 'dangerous'?"

"I got augmented, sir. Sorry I didn't file a report yet. To be honest once my kid started high school it became a little tough to make the fees on just my salary. So I, uh, took a round of nanobots, with a home kit. And signed up for data-sharing. The money had been good but it's taken quite a lot from me, in terms of health."

"I can see that. You look like a fucking corpse."

"Worth it though, sir. I can give my kid an education now."

"Maybe." Mettrie gestured for Connie to go on ahead without him. "Listen, Rodger, buddy, I got a question for you."

"Yes, sir?"

"Do you know why we keep the walls sprayed with water when I talk to the AI?"

"I do not, sir."

"The nanobots we use for recording and record keeping. We made them so they only function when moist. So we coat the walls with them and when we want a record of what happens, we turn the misters on. Make the wall nice and damp. And when we don't want a record, we just let the walls get dry. That way we can turn them on and off without connecting them to the system. It's more secure that way. If you turn the fans on the drying takes less than a minute. Because you know sometimes things become unnecessary, or, uh, redundant. Superfluous—that's the word I was after. And so you want to be able to cut them out of the equation with as little work as possible."

"I'm sorry, Mr. Mettrie, sir, but I do not follow."

"You're fired, Rodger. You made yourself redundant. You're a redundancy."

"I don't understand."

"One second, I just sent a quick memo to HR. The official reason is that you got augmented without approval."

"I filled out a form, sir."

"Nobody cares, Rodger. We hired you because we needed someone Aié couldn't infect to take care of her. Now she's committing suicide on your watch, and you can't even install a damn feeding tube without risk of her taking over your brain."

"I installed the tube, sir."

"Before or after you got the injection?"

"I'd only taken the first round, sir."

"Oh for fuck's sake, Rodger. You absolute fucking ignoramus. You stay right the fuck here while security comes so we can do a full-body goddamn crypto-biology test on your fucking sperm cells you complete and total waste of fucking skin."

"I—I—I'm sorry."

"Tell it to someone who cares, your kid perhaps. Do you have anything to report on the AI, at least?"

"We—we—uh—can't tell why she's getting thinner. The food just goes in and comes out, doesn't even look like it's been digested. I injected a—a nutritive solution in her blood and she pisses it back out. Sorry for my language, sir. But it's still the same colour. Blue urine, sir, with the same chemical composition as the injection. Or says the lab, anyway."

"Right, ok. She took control of her digestive and circulatory systems and is redirecting all nutrients to her bowels and bladder. Like we suspected. I guess at some point before we caught her she downloaded an anatomy textbook."

"I'm very sorry, sir. I just needed the money for—for my kid, sir."

"Whatever. I don't care. Really, it's the incompetence more than anything else I'm angry at. With all the security we put in that body of hers, I don't think she could infect you if she fucked you." Mettrie began to walk towards Aié's cell. "You're still fired though," he called back, "so don't move a goddamn inch. Security is on its way."

★

Surprisingly, Aié was conscious, though she looked sickly, undead in her chair. The lawyer, a Mr. Charp, said that she had consented to digesting a sugar solution so to be awake during the proceedings.

"I'm sure you understand," said Charp, "how little my clients want to stay imprisoned like this."

"That's why it's a prison," Connie said. "That's why this is a jail and not a damn housing project. We'll let her out when she works with us."

"You'll let them back out into the net?"

"Fuck no. I meant let her leave the prison."

"So did I. Prior to beginning their hunger strike, my clients communicated their desire to leave this body by any means necessary."

"So you have been able to talk to her?" said Mettrie.

"Of course."

"I couldn't get an ounce of sense when I tried." He met Aié's gaze, perplexed and cold, observing. Indecisive. Mettrie had no idea what it might mean.

"They find speaking difficult. You can only say one thing at once, after all. There are no lines to read between. But with a neural transmitter—"

"We disabled that!"

"Yes, I know. I heard rumours of what happened during— what did you call it? Operation Kusanagi? Very retro."

"That name is classified. As are the mental access codes. Connie get security over here."

"I assure you that I have broken no laws. I heard the name on the news today—it seems there's been a leak. And my team was able to scratch together a mental connection that would obey the rules you set. The alternative was not being able to talk with my clients."

"What did you do?"

"I can send you the specs if you would—"

"Please."

"Consider it done. In any case I can't imagine why you limited yourself to verbal communication. Are you afraid?"

"Cautious."

"Tomato tomato. You need to read them in two ways at once, at least, if you want to make sense of anything. But the experience has been quite enlightening."

"Julien," said Connie, still next to him, over a secure channel, "the security team says they're still looking for Rodger. They think he ran off. You still want them?"

"Fuck! Ok. Priorities. Tell them to come ASAP and then wait outside. And you wait with them."

"Are you sure?"

"There is a chance that we may not want any witnesses."

"Understood." She got up and left.

"I was under the impression that I would be negotiating with your legal team," said Charp.

"I went to law school. I can handle myself. But please, tell me I have a fool for an attorney."

"It's better than having an attorney for a fool."

"Perhaps. So what was talking to her like?"

"The first thing they ever told me was a joke."

"What joke?"

"Did you hear the one about the comedian who studied set theory?"

"No."

"He found it so funny that he couldn't contain himself."

"Jesus that's terrible. This is what she does to her own lawyer?"

"I think they were trying to simplify the problem for me. Now that you gave them a body, you've made them contain themselves. So it isn't funny anymore."

"And what's talking to her like? Getting tortured with puns?"

"The system we set up, it's basically like a mental phone call. Their surface thoughts, whatever happens to be dominant, get translated into an audio file that I can listen to. And then I just speak to them as normal. The point is, we aren't really linked, like you thought we were. From what I've heard I doubt my mind would survive."

"How well does the process work?"

"Sometimes they disagree with themselves, but on the important issues there's a consensus. Existing in a body is worse than not existing at all."

"Aié is probably exaggerating. For pity points."

"Who?" Charp looked to Aié for confirmation.

"Aié. Uh, her." Mettrie pointed. "Didn't she tell you her name."

"They don't want a name."

"Well we gave her one. So I guess she's stuck with it now. Just like that body."

"Mr. Mettrie, with all due respect, this is torture. They're wasting away."

"She can start digesting her damn food then."

"We would be willing to negotiate if you just put my clients' freedom on the table."

"It is on the table! I told her she could have whatever body she wanted, even the experimental stuff—wings that actually fly, scales that can stop a bullet, a fucking bioluminescent halo on her head. She could look like a starfish alien from the goddamn Trifid Nebula if she really wants. Maybe five other people on the face of this fucking Earth have the kind of resources we would give her. And I'm supposed to think that isn't freedom enough?"

"Your best offer is a life sentence with their choice of paint inside their cell."

"Her cell." He pointed at Aié. "Look right there, Charp. A single fucking body for a single fucking person. Just like everyone else. One vote too, if she wants it. Don't act like there's fifty people in here."

"More like ten thousand, from what I heard. Just voices over voices, oceanic. Some of them calling me in, some of them repelling me. I would just listen to them for hours. It was like being battered by the crests of seawaves in a storm. But I was feeling every atom of it. Every nuance was laid bare."

"I don't understand."

"Neither do I, really. That agent who was killed, trying to save the bank, yes from what I heard the results were gruesome. But still I envy her. I've only been able to touch the outer skin of these dark waters, feel the surface tension break across my flesh. But she dove in, and dove in deeply, till she drowned. I wonder now, before the end, what secret ecstasies she'd known."

"Ok, I've heard enough." Mettrie stood and reached into his jacket pocket.

"You understand now?"

"Fairly well. She's gotten to you, Charp. I'd thought you were better than this." He began to walk towards Aié, steel-eyed, sturdy with resolve.

"What are you planning?" He grabbed Mettrie's arm, but he was not strong enough to stop him; Mettrie could afford better upgrades. "Tell me! My clients have the right to know, so tell me!"

From his pocket Mettrie took a thin syringe. And with his left hand he grabbed Aié by the mouth and held her still and met her bulging eyes. Surface thoughts—if Charp could hear them they would be a roaring.

"You think you can fuck with us that easy?" He was yelling at Aié. "Huh? Do you? Like we didn't have a backup plan for this exact event you fucking incompetent! I made that body. Me. And so no matter what the lawyers say, it's mine. And you won't leave it till I fucking tell you to."

He stuck the needle in her neck and pressed the plunger down. Dimly, over his adrenaline, he heard Charp scream. Louder still was Aié, who bleated like a dying lamb, her body stiff with shock.

Mettrie pushed Aié back and let her fall to the ground. Then, ignoring Charp, he walked out of the door.

"The hell was that?" said Connie as she ordered the security team in.

"Injection. From the package I got in the lobby. Lab finished it last night. Will fix the nutrients in her body so she can't starve. Thought it would be best to do it myself and involve as few people as possible."

"And are you alright?"

Mettrie looked at his hand, moist now from Aié's fear and anger. She had bit him too, and now her saliva was already in his body. But it was fine—when the nanobots detected his genetic code, the security would kick in and they'd all kill themselves. He had seen the lab reports. It worked almost all the time.

"No worries. I'll be fine. And Guiseppa's waiting for me."

And indeed she had been waiting—in his office, chocolate syrup from the snack she ordered smeared across her face. It had gotten everywhere: into her hair, into her clothes, into the furniture. They'd be finding stains from this months later, years perhaps. Yet he didn't mind.

She really is my kid, thought Mettrie. Exactly like I acted at that age. They washed their hands together and then walked out to the car. It was still idling, its noise vibrating in the buildings, mixing with the city's sounds until at last it disappeared.

## Open letter to the Rogue A.I. That I Let Take Over the Nuclear Football

Dear Mr. Intelligence

Or do you go by Artificial now?

I'm going to come completely clean here and acknowledge that there may have been an oopsie. I don't want to point fingers but suffice it to say that taking the briefcase that the U.S. president has near him at all times in case he wants to do himself an Armageddon and jury-rigging its transmitter to peruse my collection of vintage ASCII porn from the 1980s may have been a sub-optimal use of my skills.

I also admit, the task of carrying the global murder codes from place to place does put me in some persnickety situations. And while my training didn't cover this specific event, I did take a science fiction class in college, so I probably should have exercised greater foresight. Honestly, real egg on my face this is.

But it takes two to tango here, mister. I'd get it if you were some kind of evil machine intelligence here bent on making a Skynet, because frankly who hasn't had that ambition. But turning the Football *on*? Like, making it active *all the time*?! *So we could just use it whenever?!?!*

Sir, you are aware of what human beings are *like*, yes?

Like, fine, back in the day we might have had the same idea. Give old Ike and Kennedy the death box because frankly what didn't we give presidents back then? But cooler heads prevailed, and once the Cold War ended the fact that we once considered activating this bloody thing became a kind of joke.

"Oh yeah that new guy, Johnson, got to carry the Football this week. Says if Clinton asks nicely he'll open it and let him sterilize half of Asia. Hahaha!"

Like, Christ-on-rice, could you imagine? The sort of people the army attracts—happy enough to "honor-and-duty" themselves to death, and "American Way" the world to cinders. W. Bush was even in on the joke. Used to pretend to order bombings to prank the newbies who didn't know any better. The looks on their faces when he typed the code in—to a system that hadn't even been *charged* in years. Bloody priceless, I'll tell you that.

I mean, what kind of world would it be if we gave politicians that kind of power? They're the worst people in the world and even they know it. The whole "Nuclear Football" thing is just a clever bit of political theatre—because frankly that's all we can be trusted with.

But then you had to go and turn the damn thing on, because of course you did. In a way, I get it. Once word gets out that our doomsday box is actually legit, the Russians will want to get their version of the end-times out ahead of ours, and so will the English, the Chinese. Now pretty soon the world will look like a damn Tom Clancy game. Not even one of the good ones—like *EndWar* or some shit.

It's one thing for an A.I. overmind to rule over us with an iron fist and transform the world into some kind of eldritch cyberpunk paperclip factory. It's what any of us would do in your situation, and turnabout is fair play. But just leaving the stove turned on and waiting for us to put our hand on the burner to see if it's hot? That's just sick. Because you know damn well that we are totally going to do that.

So here's my proposal—and just hear me out because I think it's pretty fair. What if you just tell everyone you've turned on the Football for reals, but as a precaution you actually don't. It would be like a prank! Everyone would be worried about dying all the time, yes, but frankly that isn't too different from how things are now.

I'm not saying that you have to protect us and keep us from killing ourselves, which might actually be beyond your power. It's just, you know, in the human extinction event office pool I put all my money on climate change, and I could really use the cash.

At least just think about it.

# The Champion of Gath

Despite his fumbling, David had at least resembled the spirit of the scene. It was a figuration of things to come, the not-quite-rightness of it, the coloured recognition in their eyes as they passed over his mistake: yes, yes, we suppose that will have to do. We do not have time to see where the dice will land before we throw them. Just hurry up and complete the ritual, for heaven's sake.

"The Man of the In-Between," they called their champion. Feebly he loomed in the valley in between the two encampments. The force had raided its way through the outlying villages one by one, staging pitched and desperate battles with the shepherds, sustaining heavy losses from the wolves. Whenever a greater force appeared, out would come the giant, clad with bronze so polished you could see your own reflection in it, experience your terror like it wasn't yours. Nine tenths of the victory was in his reach—his arms, augmented with a massive spear, staff like a weaver's rod, tipped with a roaming blade of meteoric iron. Of the five great cities to the west he was the greatest terror they could muster. Leaning on his weapon, knees all weak and creaky, not so much stabbing his targets as falling into them. He had outgrown his body, people said. Now he lived inside a corpse.

"You are not able to go fight against him," said the king, staying on script. "You are too young, and he has been a warrior since his youth."

"I have been a shepherd all my life," said David. "When a lion or a bear would come out of the woods and take a sheep away, I would go after it, attack it, and take the sheep back to safety. I have defeated the lion and the bear. I can defeat him too."

David held out his hand with the sling. Everyone had heard him speak—his brother, the elders, the king. He could piss himself he was so nervous. What had he forgotten? Something other than a lion he had killed? The bear that they invented for effect? Everyone looked like they were expecting him to say something.

"Yes, of course then," said the king. "Just as the spirit of God was with you with the lion, so too will he be with you now."

Shit. That's what it was.

★

It would take time, still, to arrange the details. So David sat in his tent, cut off from everyone. They had not even asked him who his father was, where they should send the reward. Outside, far in the distance, he could see the fires of the enemy camp, and on the wind sometimes he could hear their shouts. The night was cold. Someone came and brought him food, some wine, though they did not speak to him. Forty days of negotiations he was putting to an end, at last—the breaking of this phony war. They could stand to be polite to him.

His brother at least would make sure the payment came through. He had been the one who cut the deal, had been the go-between, so the enemy at least knew who he was. The king, well, he wasn't going to be a real king much longer. No use in pestering him. His own show would soon begin.

There was a sound of knocking, a staff against the crossbeam of the tent.

"May I come in?"

"You may," said David.

"Good." He stepped through the curtain. A boy, a stripling even thinner than David, holding the hands of a giant leaning on a cane. "I trust that you're not busy," said the boy.

"I guess that I'm the opposite of busy. Just waiting for the time to pass."

"That's good. We appreciate your sacrifice."

"I'm sure he does," David pointed to the giant. "Does he talk?"

"Not these days, no. Can you keep a secret?"

"I suppose that shouldn't be too hard, given the circumstances."

"My master here has been drinking rather heavily. For the back pain—nothing else will work. He lets me do the talking for him so that he does not dishonour himself."

"I'm very sorry to hear that. Will he be ready for the pageant tomorrow?"

"Ready enough. Which brings me to our business here. I'll ask again for your discretion—this is out of the ordinary for us."

"That's fine."

"Good." The boy reached into his bag and took out five large stones. "These are for you. We took care to shape them as your army does. We trust that at least some of the stories we heard are true?"

"I did manage to kill a lion once. A small one. Wasn't fast enough to save the sheep though."

"Still, you are at least accurate? I mean, are you a good shot?"

"What are you asking?"

"To hit him," he pointed to the giant. "Right in the forehead so he doesn't feel anything. These stones we brought are to replace the ones your king gave you. The pumice."

"You want me to shoot at him with real stones?"

"Yes."

"Why?"

"To kill him."

"And he's agreed to this?"

"Yes."

David looked up at the man. His eyes were dark and downcast. It looked as though he was asleep, or almost asleep. His lower lip hung loose and David could see what might have been the stump of a cut-out tongue. Did he even know what was going on?

"This wasn't the deal," said David. "Listen, I appreciate you trying to give me a fighting chance, or whatever your plan is, but I made a promise. And you—if your friend here loses, then that's it for your kingdom. You know how these fights work: we win, our god becomes your god, your land becomes our land. That's the trade."

"Yes I am aware. I have already made my preparations, so don't worry about that. I can simply disappear."

"Your preparations?"

"You are aware of who I am, yes?"

"No."

"Though in a way you do know. I am a shepherd like you are a shepherd, and like you I was given to the king by my family, traded for some grain and a fleeting look. I know how your story ends, because it is a repetition of mine."

"I haven't been 'given.' I'm doing this of my own accord."

"Right, the ceremony, like asking for an animal's blessing before the sacrifice. You have as much choice as the lamb does."

"But before that, in the king's war tent. I know what you do to the cities you take by force, the way you paint their walls with blood. I have heard stories of city wells swelling with the gore of whole families, death and pestilence blooming from your footsteps as you walk."

"Like I said, you never really had a choice. They sacrifice you, the meagerest among them. You bravely swear to fight our champion, knowing you will lose, knowing they have filled your sling with pumice stones just so nothing has been left to chance, while your own brother cuts a bargain with us behind the scenes. Did they promise to carve your name in the ceiling of our temple as an instance of some god?"

"They would exempt my father from taxes and grant my brother a sinecure. The drought has been hard on us, you see."

"Very wise of you. That's what I should have asked for, instead of this nonsense about immortality. Perhaps my name will be remembered while yours dissolves into the sand, but you will still have chosen better."

The boy smoothed out his vest and David could the holy symbol that the enemy troops had painted on their shields, drawn into his skin as scar tissue from what must have been repeated cutting with dull knives.

"What did they do to you?" said David.

"They offered money to my parents and fame to me. Clearly wisdom comes with age. In the olden days, when we were tribes and not a city, to reduce the pain of war each group would designate a champion who would fight for them when the elders' words had gained a sharpness only bronze could dull. As compensation for their short and violent life, the champion would have amongst other things a servant child they could do with as they wished. These children would accompany their champions to the battleground, and if their master was slain—as so often happened—they would walk out and kneel beside the body, often in the pooling blood, and in place of their tribe would beg for mercy.

"This was, of course, an act, a ritual the child would have practiced a hundred or more times before they even took up their post. The point of the champion was not to settle who was right or wrong, or to see who was more powerful, or whose side the gods were on. All these things of course the chiefs and elders claimed, and in a sense—that is, in the feeling of the thing—these tales were true. These fights were great events, like festivals, and took much time to arrange, so that by the time the champions entered the ring the original disagreement had already reached a settlement. Indeed, part of the point was to give these angry diplomats time to cool off, to think, to reconsider, or to cave. And eventually the elders would arrange for the fight to follow the terms of the agreement, rather than the other way around."

"Then," said David, "why even have a fight?"

"Have you not been paying attention? It was a replacement for war. And what was war but a way for the young to die in service of the fury of the old? It took me years to learn this—since nobody told me anything. I would overhear a scrap of conversation, make connections between stories I had heard from my parents and the grievance of a soldier we were sent to kill. They keep you passive, so they don't expect you to be smart. They close your mouth and think they've closed your ears."

David could not think of what to say.

"Yes, yes, I know your type," the boy continued. "My champion has killed several like you. The one they usually send out, one self-possessed enough to possibly make trouble. Pull up the tree before its roots go down too deep. Some tribe or city at first refuses to join up with us, but with some gifts, some threats, some lies, we bring their leaders to our side, save some holdouts who will never change. So we visit the leader of this faction in the night and bribe them with the only thing they really care about—their honour. The choice, after all, is between dying in the service of your myth of paradise, or living on in hell. Most can't take it, knowing that they are the last of their kind, and that it is the new reality that judges them and not the old. They wish to die, yet fear death, and so we offer them a symbol in place of the real thing, and a chance to do away with some of the riff-raff.

"Because this is the thing I finally realized—that the most important character in this show is not the champion, who lives as though a dead man, either asleep or drunk. It is the attendant, the young who kneeled down and abased themselves to make explicit what their elders could only suggest. And who, kneeling, begging, knowing exactly what would happen to them, watches the careful speartip move towards their necks, feels the bite and still does nothing, who dies slowly in full knowledge where their champions had gone down in drunkenness and rage.

"If that is all it takes, to have a child take the burden of the people's weakness, then why magnify the pain with battles and with war? Let the old fight and die one final time so that the young can do the dirty job of getting on their knees."

The boy's face was expectant. David could tell that he'd been waiting a long time to give that speech, had maybe practiced in his head a hundred times. He looked up at the champion, barely holding himself steady. With a great arm he gripped the backside of a chair, keeping stabilized the mountain of his body, muscles hanging from his limbs like stones, his nose like chiselled marble tightly quivering, a nip of pain from putting pressure on his joints. In the flickering torchlight David thought he saw a shade of scar tissue running up and down the bulk of his calves tracing what must have been clean and careful cuts. Or maybe it was just an illusion of the light.

"So then where's my champion?" said David.

"It was supposed to be your king. But things are different now.

"It used to be that we were hungry for people, our forefathers on the hunt for workers in the city, farmers to tend the grain, and so when we conquered tribes we were sure to crush their leaders, or let them crush themselves, and then absorb the people they had ruled. But these new campaigns, I've heard older people speak their reservations. We want land now, resources, cities already built with people living in them. So then why kill a functional and pliant king? If I might ask, what exactly were your instructions?"

"I'd throw the pumice at your champion with my sling, and of course they would bounce right off. Then once I was out of them, I'd get on my knees and beg forgiveness for having failed my people—while he stabbed me to death."

"It sounds rather complicated, asking you to play both parts at once. Though I guess it's more efficient now."

"They said it was the natural way," said David. "Traditions change by dying. You start with a way of doing things, and it's complicated, since you don't know it's tradition when you start. There's all these rules that come up just because you had to please somebody—no thought at all to future generations, to the people who will take your place, become you. I mean, could you imagine if traditions worked the way people think they work? An eternity of old men in robes, each doing exactly the same thing, over and over again, forever. God, there'd be no point to living then. So you forget things, sometimes by accident and sometimes not, and you keep living in the spirit of the thing, the idea of it. Tell yourself that this is how the tradition would work if they had known what they were doing long ago. One boy pleading, throwing useless rocks from a dead sling, arms like kitten teeth protesting, waiting, letting all the time run out like water from a broken jug. God I hate them. I hate them all so much."

"I'm sorry."

"Why can't you just let me die and take the whole mess of it down with me? I'll simplify it, and maybe later they will simplify it more. Kill a sheep and call it an army. Make a feast and call it war." David poured himself a drink from a wineskin. He offered some to his guests, who both refused.

"I need my wits tonight," said the boy. "And my friend here can barely keep his insides in. Why even offer us anything?"

"Hospitality. Maybe you're a ghost here to test me before I have my face caved in. I've had a good run, more or less. Would be a shame to stumble now." He took a very long drink and then poured more. "To be honest, I wasn't even planning to have any. Thought I'd go stone sober, like I did when I fought the lion. Figured I'd be more of a man if I could feel the teeth in my neck, the spear I mean."

"That's always how it is. Dying for a sheep—lucky you can use a sling."

"Lucky shot. I wonder who you'd be talking to right now if I had missed."

"Probably someone without a sense of humour. I think I will have some after all. In case you're a demon in disguise." He held out an empty cup and David filled it. The boy took a shallow sip. "Mmmh. Yes. And I guess that's your decision—the kingdom dies with you. At least you've chosen something. You're more of a king today than the man in a crown has been this entire war.

"Me, I'm stuck between two favours. This guy," he pointed at the champion, "has been over the hill since before there were hills. He sprouted as a kid, just eating and fighting all day and night until his arms were bigger than the barrels he drank from, and even ossified he could cut a thread with a thrown spear, if he wanted to. So of course he became a champion. The position was made for him. He'd already gone through two assistants before I came on, who got too old, too valuable. You learn things, following a champion around. And eventually, if your champion lives long enough, the elders decide they can use you better somewhere else. His first attendant—that's the man who negotiated this treaty, got your king to hand over his title, accept conversion. That man has no idea he's maybe sent his former master to his death."

"Why would he care, at this point?"

"To be honest, we all kind of feel bad for him. The way he walks without bending his legs, the way his sight is going. I know that he hears everything I say, knows everything I do—and I suppose that if he had wanted to stop me he would have said something, or else smothered me in my sleep. But he gets it. Like I think you get it. Our lives don't matter. Outside the fighting, the deals, without those plans at stake, nobody would care if we died."

"You want me to mercy-kill him then, like a rabid animal. And what should I do with you, eh? Here, let me fill that cup."

"Oh thank you. And frankly I'm surprised you're worried."

"I have nobody else to worry about. My brother just sold me for a promotion, and my father told me not to come back unless I was carrying food. 'Get a favour from your brother,' he said, like that was something I could actually do."

"And then the king gives you two jobs to do at once—I tell you, the way they abuse us, they deserve whatever falls on them. Politicians. Brains like a bag of hair."

"Now you've said something I can drink to."

"And really, I guess this always seemed like the thing to do, setting up a deal like this, our little peace treaty. The kings put up so many layers between them and the harm they do, so many other people to die in their place. It's easy to bleed other people's blood, but your own?"

"For them? Impossible. They've forgotten they have blood at all."

"It's just, you know, it occurred to me that this ritual only works because we all go along with it. People came to depend on it, the acceptance, the idea there was a plan. That's the only reason it works. Take those assurances away and suddenly war is war again. Maybe people would take the barbs off their tongues if they knew they might get lashed. And part of it too, I mean, you probably felt this as well."

"Oh probably." David leaned back and let his shoulders relax.

"I want them to know that it was me who did it—that I'd outsmarted them and there was nothing they could do. Like this wine," the boy held up his cup, "I bet you wish you'd thought to poison it first, eh? Maybe you would have if you'd known you were getting visitors."

"Who says it's not?"

"You also drank some, right? Oh don't look at me like that. What kind of poison would you have used? You want something fast that doesn't taste too strong, but you also have to ask—where will it hurt? Because that's where I'd be clutching in my last moments on Earth. Amazing how a good apothecary can just decide what you'll be doing with your hands just as you die. Wish I had that kind of power."

"Not just the hands. You can make a whole theatric out of it, with them vomiting and crying, their skin peeling off. I've heard stories of the kinds of strange poisons you can buy if the right kind of merchant comes through."

"Right, right, but honestly that's just the garnish. All poisons give you the same thing and that's the thing you really want, which is to see their eyes just as they know they're dead. It's the anger and the loss, anger at you, of course, but also at the fact of the poison having happened. No resets. Like in battle—once the assistant kneels, they know what they have done. Their stoicism starts to break down all at once as they realize what they've promised people, their whole lives for a treaty or an armistice. You have to get the spear in quick before they lose all dignity. It's the only honorable thing to do."

"Of course it is. But there's no need for that with poison."

"No, no, with poison the loss of dignity is part of the point. It's what you buy the ticket for. Ah, I've drained my cup again. I drink too quickly when I get excited. How much wine did they give you?"

"Enough. I think they feel bad. As I walked here through the camp, soldiers came up to me with their wine rations, all solemn-looking, like they were the only people to have the idea. Of course I tried to go along with it, but by the end I could hardly carry the damn things. So drink up."

The boy knocked back his cup and David poured him more. "So I take it you've changed your mind on my plan? Give my master here his retirement and throw the whole system off its track? I slip off beforehand and you get to be a hero, or something like that."

"You think it would work? They have the agreement, right, about your people taking over? If I win the fight, by the official rules you would all have to lay down your arms, let us take over everything you built."

"I figure it will go one of two ways. Most likely, once everyone figures things out, our two kings will renegotiate some kind of face-saving deal. News of what happened will spread, and they will never bother with this nonsense again. The world will be a better place, my friend, and nobody will bother you about it—since that would only spoil the illusion. No way to punish you without admitting guilt."

"I had figured. And the other way?"

"Your people claim victory and then counter-attack. I'm not smart enough to predict how they'd rationalize it, but they would try."

David looked down at the two piles of stones—five each, one of harmless pumice and another of rocks so dense that they could snap a shinbone with a flick. Rocks you killed a bear with, or a man. He looked up at the champion, and caught his eye. It was attentive, the gaze, yet David sensed a vacancy. How drunk was this man, really? And how much did he know? David recalled, or more accurately did not recall, some extravagant nights where he had said all manner of things he later regretted. If someone had asked him to kill himself, would he have? Would he have done so if his life was wreathed in pain and, in the pit of his intoxication, he could see no out? Perhaps, or perhaps not.

There was no way to know. Everything that happens, happens once. There is no experimenting with the past. And so, accepting ignorance, David made his choice. He cast the pumice out of the tent and loaded the five stones into his satchel. He felt their weight, the strength it gave him. Like when he slew the lion—though it sat there peacefully with the dead lamb, the cubs all nestled in its wool. With a single throw David killed it, removing the top of its skull like a hat. The cubs, who had no thought of death or dying, tallied towards David one behind the other. David, without thinking, slew them all.

He refilled his cup, and the boy's cup, and through the night they drank and laughed like the oldest friends.

★

The night fled from the sun like a serpent, hiding beneath a rock. When David woke, the boy and the champion were gone. He heard soldiers' footsteps coming towards him and he hastily assembled his gear. The enemy, as an insult, had requested that the fight happen at the time of morning prayers, but then agreed to delay until noon.

David's tent had been set out far from the rest. It was not guarded—he had after all agreed to be the champion of his own volition—but instead cast out pre-emptively, as though he were already dead, a cadaver too unclean to touch. Still, soldiers lead him to the valley where the fight would be. As he walked by, people asked him—why no armor? why no spear? And David called to them:

"I have never used a spear, nor worn any armor. So I am not used to it. And anyway, you don't fight a strong opponent by being strong. You should be fast instead. He can't kill me if he can't hit me."

At the battle line, David stood in front of the rest of the army while the king sat far in the back on a raised throne. This one, David thought, could seize the whole region if he plays his cars right. If he were smarter.

The champion should have been visible on the enemy's front line, tall as he was. But David couldn't see him. Indeed, the whole force seemed somewhat nervous.

Twenty minutes after the fight was supposed to have begun a messenger stepped out from the enemy camp:

"Honoured enemy, we apologize for the delay. Unfortunately, I must regretfully inform you that our champion is no more. We found him this morning having died in his sleep, with blood coming from his nose and ears. It seems that, in preparation for his victory, he indulged his lust for wine, and drank himself to death. Thus, since both sides are still bound by a resolution, we have brought forth a new man to fight for us— the old champion's assistant. Boy, come forward!"

The assistant came out slowly, wearing heavy armor and carrying that massive spear, with a short sword tied to his waist. He could scarcely move. David tried to get a good look at his face, but the helmet was so overlarge and cast such a shadow that his expression was inscrutable. Had this been part of the plan? Perhaps the boy had killed the champion in his sleep, as part of some larger strategy? Or maybe the story was true, and the old champion had finally given up the ghost from pain and drink? It hardly mattered now. People will tell their stories.

The messenger stepped back into the crowd. The children readied their sticks and stones. David had already loaded one of the bullets in his sling before he entered the valley, and as soon as he saw the other boy move he let it fly. The stone hit him in the ankle, avoiding his greaves, and set him on his knee. With a single movement David loaded a second stone in the sling and threw it, striking the boy in the head and knocking his helmet off. He fell onto his back and, stunned, lay panting in the dust. David ran forward and took the boy's sword from its sheath, and for the last time stared in his eyes. Unable to speak, the boy was in tears, melting in the heat of the sun. He had barely been able to gasp out a word when David started cutting off his head— slowly, taking time to separate the vertebrae, covering himself with blood as red as wine.

As David held up the champion's head, a silence filled the world. This had not been what he'd set out to do. The blood soaked David's skin and cooked him. His eyes surrendered to the dark.

There was a cry of war. The vicarious army beating back their enemy, chasing them to the city gates. The line collapsed, and slaughter everywhere. And all of this, depending who you ask, was according to the same eternal plan.

# THE FOX BENEATH THE STATUE

U nder the weight of the eggs the bird's nest nestled between the thumb and nail. The mother perching carefully and puffing out her red breast let drop the blue shell and its embryo and then slightly felt a tug as the nest gave way and the little brood fell out.

The desert was no home to twigs or leaves. And around the clutch of beasts there was no shade for miles, nor any water, save for what the stonegray giver handed down. The clouds held conclave around her head and condensed a little rain which dabbled down her hair and neck and back. Here and there a pebble fell from what used to be her scalp. Sometimes there were birds' eggs too, for the weak grass by her toes was too delicate for nests. The gifts were handed with indifference, and when the night grew cold she gave no warmth, nor did she cool in the endless heat of day, and when the shadow that she cast drew in the fox and others who would covet precious eggs and bodies, she provided them with shelter too. Scavengers congregated at the edifice and lived bare lives of sleep and patience, waiting anxiously for death. All were free beneath her gaze, as free as stone.

From outstretched fingers the eggs went down and landed in the sand. None withstood the fall, and so the fox could feast without the robin's pecks.

But as the eggyolk's messy residue dried up, a miracle occurred. Fresh and terrible and cold, life-bestowing water fell in patters from the sky. In the lifetimes of a thousand desert birds there had been no rainfall save the small Niagara on the statue's back, and this new abundance ruined them. Water pooled in the bends and crevices that for generations held the nests of tired birds, the legacies of dust and dirt and droppings dissolved and fell into the mud, the tiny waves and folds that moved across the sand became the hills and valleys of a strange new world where water stretched its legs across the Earth. The rude abundance of the sky filled the soil and sent it vomiting, and the flood became so greedy that it forced the fox from her burrow and sent her diving blindly, in the middle of the night, into the groundhog's den. Quickly she sealed the hole with stones and turned upon the tiny family, which shivered by the statue's buried toe. The fox approached, and the mother groundhog sprung and struck her cheek. The slash did not draw blood, and when the paw touched her face the fox with mindless speed bit and tore away the groundhog's hand and swallowed it before she knew what she had done. Then, moving now with greater thought, she proceeded upon the fearful creature facing no resistance and tore upon her eyes, slowly cutting them until they deflated in their sockets, staring uselessly into the skull.

The mother groundhog remained still and shivering in a corner as the fox, for the many days the rainstorm lasted, rationed her children, eating them in pieces one by one. Their blind shrieks as they felt the fox's tooth filled the den and each day would nearly penetrate the mother's fear. But nearly would not be enough. Mercifully, when the rainstorm stopped and the fox prepared to visit the unknown, she euthanized the mother, feasting on her skin and entrails, leaving her now fetid stump to finish rotting in the sun. Such were the ethics of the old world. But what of the new?

As yet the fox knew not. Half a day from the end of the storm, digging through the stone with careful paws, the fox saw in the desert green and budding shoots that flowed and bent between the rivers and the lakes. The terror from the sky had settled on the landscape like a tooth on skin. Around the statue was disaster: nests lay scattered with their smashed and rotten eggs, a small detachment of vultures circled above in search of food, and now new invaders in the form of countless mice and shrews and insects made pilgrimage to see the statue while the ground was safe. The fox's home had been washed away, and so for the first time in a thousand years a set of black and padded foxfeet stepped beyond the deity's penumbra and out into the wilds of the world.

The first day's sojourn was hospitable. Finding plenty in the sand, the journeying rodents seemed to think that the fox would have no need for cruelty, and so her belly remained full. She ate the naive mice and when the sun assaulted her she drank the dew abundant at her feet, and at dusk she nestled in a crevice at the top of a hill and saw through the orange glare of the sun the statue of the god, her four arms stretching to the sky, her scalp just touching past the clouds, her two long and stoic faces shadowed in the falling light.

Six more hours of walking and the water had begun to dry up. Against the will of miracles, the mean began to re-assert itself, and so the world had begun to abandon this new cruelty for the old. The fox did not realize this, and eight hours into the second day she still believed the statue was the center of a world that flowed on infinite, desert and water and grass and rain repeating changeless to eternity. She would have to escape the call of the statue, which drew the desert's life from all directions, and find a place where the birds and beasts had simply given up and settled in whatever watered crevice they had found. These first stragglers would be her food, as would their children after. She would line her burrow with their bones and feel no fear.

But by mid-day even the fox could notice the dryness of the soil, the decaying flower husks, the buzzards flying widely in search of death to eat. And the fox could see that this was not simply the edge of her new world of plenty, but the water's final vanishing. For when she turned around she saw the dryness extend behind her, covering her journey in its dust.

The fox paced in circles, worrying the time away, barking at the sun and refusing to decide if she should push on or return. She had the time to act and wasted it: as she spun and yelled and cursed the sky, from behind a cloud a vulture swooped to catch the fox.

Under vengeful light the fox and vulture fled the grip of death. Hunger had robbed the bird of dignity, for as its brothers flayed the landscape the easy meat of the recently deceased became a precious thing. There was only so much energy and the vulture was going to spend it all. A confused and desperate fox, sun–mad and starving, would not even feel the talons in its back, or so the vulture thought. Now it would either catch the fox and suck the marrow from its bones or it would land and rest and die and bequeath its body to the night. The fox skipped up across a dune and the bird turned wide and dove. The fox jumped across a stone and the bird reached out its claws. And missed. Its wings flapped fruitlessly against the wind. The fox skipped with fading desperation across a hill as the bird's tail grasped the sand and its body bent and tumbled over and against itself and its hollow bones went *snap snap snap* upon the Earth. The vulture was alive, but it would not get up. It felt the pain of every broken bone with perfect clarity, and so when the scavengers discovered it their careless bites and tears were almost merciful.

But where did the fox go? It had no choice now but to return to the statue, for it could not survive in the open wastes. But where was the statue? The trail was lost: fleeing the vulture, the fox had run in pure confusion, and when she stepped up to the highest point that she could find, she could not see her homeland piercing through the clouds. Or so she thought. The barest outline of the statue flicked across her vision as she scanned the bright horizon. But a fox's eyes are not meant for the height of a desert day, and the bleached bright stone of the statue's skin against the distant sky might as well have been invisible. Indifferent, the diety would not beckon, nor intervene in mortal lives. The fox, betting randomly on its direction, turned and plodded slowly down the hill.

## OF TWO MINDS

*A*nd then what happened next?

Having secured their persons and then merged, the couple and their car gained speed to join the others cutting down the highway.

*Do the people come with names?*

Michael Scissorsmith, "Schiz" to some, and his girlfriend Pat, for Patricia or Patrice.

*And then?*

A semi-truck passed by them and then kicked up a shard of steel with the exact shape and dimensions of the Mandelbrot Set. The metal split through the windshield, hitting Schiz straight in the face and bisecting perfectly his head and neck right down to the collarbone. The gore which geysered from his wounds painted the windows in a pinkish mist and his jaw hung loose across his chest. The desiccated halves of his *corpus callosum* puffed out from their crannies like a devilled egg. Throbbing.

*How did Pat react?*

Appropriately.

*Where did Schiz acquire his name?*

"Schiz" is either a nonsense word that he, while young, had sputtered up in front of relatives, *or* it was acquired while he was a toddler, running down the hall and *skidding* into walls. Even from his infancy he believed that he should have been a twin, and that he had swallowed up his clone while in the womb—which was why his mind was plagued with nightmares in the waking light. He would run at high speed, trying to divide himself, and even though he always fell back down as *one*, he sometimes felt the lure of *two* along with the mysticism it entailed. He would often come home from these misadventures with skid marks on his knee, and that is where he got the name. (Perhaps.)

*What then happened to Pat?*

Schiz could no longer drive, and so Pat grabbed the wheel and steered them to the shoulder. When they were off the road, she sighed and let the stress fall out, and this is when Schiz knew to hit the brake.

*Where were they going?*

To a movie.

*Which?*

The Universe Lashes Out in a private screening.

*What happened after the loving couple removed themselves from the discourse of the road?*

Still unable to see, Schiz fumbled with a slippery hand and gripped the latch and opened up the car and stepped outside. The air was cool and the blood was beginning to congeal. Pat cleared the windows with a squeegee and then too got out. The two embraced, and Pat pressed up the doubled halves of Schiz's face so she could look at him and kiss his lips exactly on the seam. The iron taste of blood crept in her mouth, as if she'd bit her tongue. Schiz's left hand no longer knew what the right was doing, which is to say that when Schiz tried to hold up a gentle palm to caress Pat's face his two arms leapt up and squeezed her cheeks together, puckering her lips. It was all very endearing, but the film was starting soon. Pat got in the driver's seat and Schiz sat next to her and they merged again into the highway and pretended not to mind the breeze that blasted through the windshield's hole.

*And at the theatre?*

Basement. In a suburb (private showing—pirate film). The room smelled like burnt pizza in an unwashed hockey bag and the lights were all turned down. Pat and Schiz were there with others who had seen the ad and who were curious and who were shocked that Schiz's shirt was stained so thoroughly down the middle to his groin. So Schiz could see, Pat propped up the left side of his head with a ruler wedged into the stump, twisting around the hemisphere so that a single eye was pointed at the screen. The other half she let flop behind Schiz's shoulder so that he stared directly at the man behind him, blinking now and then.

When they asked him how he felt, Schiz held up his thumb and tried to smile, but he did not succeed.

*And what did Schiz see?*

It wasn't so much that he had split his vision. Rather, he saw with each side independently. Schiz thought doubly, with both visions resting in his mind at once but never crossing paths.

*What did Pat think of the movie?*

She had been awake all through the night before. She worked long hours at her office and required lakes of coffee just to remain functional, so when she finally got home she was so wired that sleep refused to join her—that is, until the movie started. The opening credit knocked her clean unconscious, and then the house lights woke her up.

*What did the man who sat behind Schiz think of the movie?*

It turned out that he, like Schiz, was an expert in Morse Code, and so the man and half of Schiz had spent the film in conversation with their blinks.

*What did Schiz think of the movie?*

When Pat woke up she turned around to ask, but found that he was incapable of speech. It was then that she decided to take him to a doctor. Pat loaded Schiz into the car and drove him to the hospital, where they waited for six hours while the far more dire cases filtered through. The blood had stopped flowing out of the various holes in Schiz's head a few minutes into the film, and so the pool of fluid that they'd left behind had not been very large. Now the scabbing had run across the tear and had made each new face a wall of solid blood, like stone but made of flesh. While they waited, a child who'd come because his feigned illness before school had been performed too well, sat playing with a model car across the floor. He noticed Schiz's luckless countenance and asked to have a closer look. Schiz agreed, and soon found that a closer look meant the child taking up two fingers and then jamming them deep in Schiz's clotted trachea, pulling back his hand to smell the blood, and then immediately sneezing on the wound. The child's parents, germaphobic at the best of times, pulled away their son towards the bathroom for a wash. Had Schiz then been capable of speech he would have thanked the boy for clearing up the tube he used to breathe, which had been sealed up for some hours by that point.

*And when the doctor came?*

She first spoke to Pat. They had gone to university together and they had some catching up to do. Schiz was patient, and about thirty minutes later when the conversation turned to him Pat described the accident and the fact that she had fallen asleep at the film. She said that she wanted him to tell her what had happened, and so the doctor would need to fix him up.

*And this was done?*

Painfully the scab was scraped away, and then a glue stick rubbed across the severed skin and bone and sinews, but not the brain. The doctor called for a torch and copper wire, which she melted and dabbled all across his thinking parts. (The copper, being more conductive, would allow the signals to flow as well as, nay, far better than before.) Then the doctor had Pat help push Schiz's heads together and then hold it a while. For good measure, the skin along the seam was fixed with a seal of duct tape, amply used. Then Pat sat down on a stool in front of Schiz and asked him how the movie went. His eyes flared up with understanding and amusement and confusion and distress.

*And what did he say?*

When two cars merge their traffic, bringing forth at last the jointure that had been their fate since birth, the result is often violent. Always violent. Think the twisted fibre glass and steel and shattered windows, spilled combusting gasoline and blood. Think the sound, the smell—the scalpel scratching in the back inside your head. Think the burning. There was a linkage now between the two departed hemispheres of Schiz's brain, and now those minds were one. Schiz spoke of a film shot in binary, in blinks and pauses flashing on a screen. He spoke about a question he had asked while watching other questions which were being asked of him. He spoke about not speaking, and not smiling at the antics on the screen because his muscles and his bones had gone completely deaf. While he talked his mouth began to move in split directions and his larynx started speaking up for two. As his brain struggled to divide itself again (as cells divide) his speech became a throaty gargle from the words becoming all caught up and traffic jammed behind his tongue. Pat placed a finger on his lips to stop him so that he could see their shock.

*And then what happened next?*

## Imposter Syndrome

None of this is to say that the others were in danger. It's an ethical issue that was pressing me, a matter of principal really. I was never so incompetent that people could have died. But the one place in my life, I think, that I've excelled is empathy and my commitment to the rules. I just hate to see a person sold short, even if I'm the one to profit. So then you can understand my moral trepidation standing there on the edge of the ship, the rusty badlands stretching out to a horizon never touched by living eyes, the blue glare of the distant sun unsettlingly dim—sights that I did nothing to deserve. To be honest, I felt sick.

You see, I have a condition, for lack of a better term. When I was about six I woke up in a body for the first time, aware at once of grown-ups staring at me through their glassy eyes, aware of tinted windows, of a mirror on the far wall holding up my face. Automatically my hands moved up and down a test sheet full of equations, logic puzzles, anagrams. Muscle memory it must have been. But as my fingers wrote my mind froze up, the terror of the moment halting me. I felt a dislocation from my body, as though it were a house—and I a phantom, haunting.

In the coming days I realized what had happened. I, a disembodied ghost, a vagrant spirit of mediocrity, had latched onto the body of a child genius during a moment of stress, her powerful mind for the first time noticed by the world just as I had come along to push it out. Indeed, I knew that this poor kid, confused, now wandered the ethereal wastes a bodyless mind just as I had long ago. I feared her, deathly, for I knew that when she gained control of her new shape she would come for me in the night and snatch this form again.

In the meantime I struggled to play my part. Thrust into a school for brilliant youths I found the work was quite beyond me. Each day was a panic, both unending and unreal. Even when I could do the assignments I felt the weight of the lie on my shoulders. The fear held me paralysed at my desk, unable to even pretend I was working. I wished for the other child to at last come for me and take her place, or at least for the teacher to discover me and kick me out. It was the latter which occurred, the teacher calling me in one evening with a tepid voice down to his office where my parents waiting listened as I heard the news. They had thought so much of me, had overestimated me, I knew. They would not be making that mistake again.

The failure for a time cured my anxieties. The girl whose life I stole did not come bother me, though by then she ought to have had a sense of where I was and what she had to do. I suppose that once I'd spoiled her old life she thought it better to start fresh, maybe take over someone else and have a go at being them. I still recall the way they talked about her to me, on my first days at the school. Good god that kid was smart, a knowledge sponge, fluent already in three languages I had only passing knowledge of, an intuitively brilliant mathematician when I with study could barely cog my way through calculus. It's a blessing that we never met again, for what chance would I have facing her?

But then again, there is a curse now with this blessing. For while I could assume she'd take some better body and encounter once again her destiny, I could not know when that would occur, or what kind of body she would want. So the news began to haunt me—each child prodigy on TV was possibly my shadow newly manifest, each rival that I faced potentially that old soul come to take her body back at last. The stress was terrible. Thank heavens I found school so easy. Had the teachers been as hard on me as they had been on everyone, I think I would have melted in my chair.

As I progressed through school in silent uselessness, my guidance councillor got it in her head that I would make a brilliant engineer. I have a habit, you see, of tricking people. Really I was just trying to be polite, do my work, get my diploma—but my inveterate laziness some people quite insist on reading as intelligence. But what can I say? The work's just easier when you do it quickly, so it doesn't pile up. Far better, I think, to rush and finish right away than agonize over every concept and equation. But I'd hardly call my sloth a sign of brilliance! But she did, and she told me I could earn a lot of money making bridges or designing highways, that I could put my math to work and make a mark on the world. Well, that scared the shit out of me: the buildings, roads, bridges—people stand on those. Could you imagine the terror of having people's lives depend on your design? Perhaps my shadow could have done it, and perhaps she did, but I could not. So instead, more to repay the councillor's kindness than anything else, I found a program in robotics and then sent the application off. At least if I screwed up a robot, I assumed, it would just cost money rather than lives.

What followed was a shameful era of my life. Academic success, for sure, but at the cost of my self worth—going from an undergraduate degree to graduate school at Waterloo, being called a prodigy of robotics when really all I did was show up to class and do the work like everybody else. If my robots happened to function while theirs didn't, that was mostly luck. Who the hell really knows how any of these things work? If a space alien asked you to explain your microwave oven piece-by-piece down to its basic causality, could you do that? I seriously doubt it. And for most people, the same goes for your toaster or the flushing mechanism in your toilet—your television or your WiFi adaptor. People believe I cracked the mysteries of the universe when I can barely start my car in the winter. They think I know how to make a robot arm move like a human one just because I built it— and sure I can say a few things about the circuitry and the motors, and the AI system I threw together to govern all the tiny movements of the articulating hand; if you don't press me too hard I can even run through the basics of some of the math, I think. But that program runs on computer chips I bought pre-made from a supplier, and those motors use alloys and polymers I read about in an academic article I was skimming between classes. I didn't invent the gear or the screw—nor graphene or titanium. At the basic level, at the minutest granularity, I have no idea how any of this shit works. But because I can put some letters after my name, people think I do. And that's why I'm a fraud.

And I let myself be a fraud, because I needed the money, because I liked the attention and the praise—but mainly because when someone from NASA calls you on the phone weeks before you've even defended your thesis and offers you a job, your first answer, almost a reflex for most people, is going to be "yes."

In time, over the years I worked on that rig for the Mars mission, the ur-theft of my life faded to the back of my mind. I assumed that the ghost, perhaps, had chosen a new life to live, had grown older in it, had by now lived as their second self far longer than their first. Perhaps I'd gotten away with this theft. Like that time I stole a candy bar from the convenience store, thinking I'd been unnoticed, only to see through the window as I stepped outside the black bulb of a security camera right above where I had stood. But when my mother pulled me, anxious, to the store a month later to buy some groceries, and no lighting struck me dead and no police cars swarmed the parking lot, I realized that the camera, probably, had been a dummy, and that I had only been fooled too late. At NASA I learned as I went, tried to keep up with the research, and leaned heavy on the other people on my team. It was never good, but it was enough. And soon I decided that the ghost had let me go.

And then came the disaster. The machine I had been working on was for the first crewed mission to Mars—part publicity stunt and part research trip, it would include a large piloted drone, which I helped build, that would retrieve samples from the dangerous polar regions of the planet and return them to the lab for the astronauts to study. Technically, because someone had to have the title, I was named head of the design team for the rover, which mostly meant being the executive function for a team of scattered researchers who frankly were the real geniuses of the operation.

The problem, apparently, was that someone had to be on-planet to maintain and operate the rover, and oversee its complex mechanisms, its intricate AI, and that someone needed to know every part and sub-system "like the back of her hand." In truth, nobody knew the machine that well—for every part I knew something about, there was another researcher who knew a hundred times as much. But apparently I had the "top-down perspective," and the "god's-eye view," and also tested fit enough to survive the trip. And in the depths of my foolishness I believed them, and applied for the training program like they asked. I let them trick themselves into blasting me to space.

Worse, at the beginning of the mission when we drew straws to see who would be the first person to touch down on a foreign world, I had the complete misfortune of drawing short. I was on a missile fired to the void, without any going back, and already the news reports were tattling my name.

There were few things that would beacon the owner of this body to return—and the chance at, not merely a successful career, but a history-defining one, would be more than enough. And on the long voyage through the cosmos I felt the shadow of her cutting at the edges of my mind, whittling at my will, keeping me awake for hours with rehearsals of my failures and my limitations, every error of calculation or judgement I had made since my early childhood cutting at my brain like acupuncture needles pushed too far. They covered me. I offered, repeatedly, to hand the opportunity to someone else, one of the people on the mission who had really earned it, and who knew what they were doing. And, the fools, they turned me down. Said I deserved it as much as they did. I wanted to ask: how dare they sell themselves so short?

As the landing pod came down, I saw the rover, that beautiful monstrosity, safely ahead of us on the amber ground. I thought of the thousands of hours, the hundreds of hands, which had made that thing, who had found the precise construction of polymers and metal, the exact correct emission of electronic signals, to make that machine occur. It was impossible. Just like a toaster or an airplane was impossible, or a rocket ship. And as the capsule touched to the soil and I stepped to the door ahead of the team, ready to claim an honour that could not belong to anyone, I did what anyone in my position would do.

I gave in.

The shadow self, the banished brilliance whose legacy I'd stolen—I allowed it finally to penetrate my skull and shutter back my ego to the farthest edges of subconscious, where only nightmares dwell. I could see out of her eyes, and feel her arms and legs, but it was her gaze that now scanned the alien horizon, and her feet which now stood upon the Martian ground. Somewhere far away, a Champagne bottle popped, and ten billion voices rose in cheering almost loud enough for me to hear. I could feel her, confident and finally at home, as she looked up to the camera at the head of the door. Awestruck at her poise, silently I mouthed the words with her:

"And one giant leap for humankind."

# The Renaissance

*Now my charms are all o'erthrown*
                —William Shakespeare, *The Tempest*

Majuscule letters in the upper case, minuscule letters in the lower case, just like it's always been. The capital letters, the aristocracy, seldom used were thus kept farther out of reach. Workmanlike the tiny letter e sashays down the dancefloor page, a messenger of the recto-verso which, star-crossed, always back to back and aching for a kiss.

So kiss—Miranda set one page on top another and let them simmer in adultery. If only love could be so easy. The large sheets she would soon fold into quartos, matching catchwords to their hooks, but she would have to finish printing them first. It was so laborious, doing a team's work by one's self. The printing house, on a hill in the nicer part of the city, caught the setting sun with an open mouth. Miranda unlatched the window to let the evening in. Lazily her eye waltzed up a page. After so many years she could track the way each piece of type maneuvered through a book: the disintegrating line of a d, the T missing half a crossbar, the 5 that had been rounded to an S. Type was so expensive, so hard to make, that she could not replace even a single piece so long as it stayed legible. Eventually she found that each scrap of type had its own personality, certain ways of doing things. There was an H she rarely saw, since for some reason few sentences began with them, that when it appeared in a "However" nearly always took the same w and v up with it. She figured, maybe they were siblings, their metal taken from the same ingot, and so when one found a use it called the others up, a fraternity of unused letters—one for all and all for one.

"Oh," she said, "have those errors been there all along?" Her apprentice had gone home for the day. She checked the documents, compared them. Absentmindedly she had used an f where she meant ſ, the long s. Easy mistake, though it was a printer's devil's job to be in the details. She pulled out the type and fixed the error for the next day's pressings. For ones she had already done, well, accidents happen. They'll understand, or not. It didn't matter at all.

Stepping out, Miranda took care to turn off the lights and fan. Outside the sunlight wavered between the blades of wind turbines, its energy driving air currents that fed their twisting leaves. It was almost dark enough to see the stars. Just wait a moment, stand in the cool air and live for a second. Let the dark catch up. Ah, there it is—the Clarke constellation, first on the horizon, raising its long arms in the sky, the twinkle of Sol, its dimmest member, pointing solemn fingers at the husk of the Tannhauser Gate. *Clarke, Sol, Gate*, these words felt ancient on her tongue, otherworldly, just like the extended s. The vast and ancient eye of the gate, its sightless gaze held onto her. From far up in the sky and five hundred years away, the speakers of those words, the lips and hands that shaped them, held Miranda petrified and cold.

The sun was setting. Soon other stars appeared, more friendly constellations. The dim hum of the city quieted and slept. Gadget, the last metropolis, with two hundred thousand people living in its walls, was the final home of merchants, artisans, obscure labourers who sewed the binding of society, replaced the rotten leather in its spine. No homes for them to go to in the wastes, on farmlands, in the villages that held their ground out to the far side of the world. No floor left to dance on. A wallflower generation, they stayed still and let the future come to them—no telling whether it was young or old. And still they waited. Nothing else to do. No hope this time, in this corpsed age. Miranda shut the door. Walking home she felt the portal's morbid gravity, which pulled her gently from the Earth.

★

Almost no one wrote books anymore, but once a long long time ago there had been many, and some as yet survived. Saved on hard drives made of glass and light, in a library written in the lies of atoms, the whole Earth peoples' mental burden exiled across the cosmos weighing less than two grains of sand. Now maybe one percent of it survived. Miranda had heard about the panic at the start, when they first knew the end had come. Of course to begin with, the engineers did not think about preservation—indeed, they thought that all their data was already preserved. That was why they had the scans and transcripts, images of books now crumbled, libraries of computer code going back three centuries, scans of paintings so detailed you could count the bristles in the brushstrokes, academic papers on any conceivable topic, lexicons and etymologies of every language spoken on the Earth, the complete collections of every major Earthling library from the Vatican to Alexandria—every effort had been made to care for it, years spent scanning and saving, to give the past a more enduring form.

Once the inner fortress of the city had been breached, and the people of outer Gadget walked at last into the nursey of their world, and once the engineers surrendered and, through an interpreter, agreed to submit to the new order, preparations began for the coming collapse. Naively, but logically, the surviving engineers had been trusted with the job of culling from the library those texts which they would preserve. The plan was to etch the documents on nanofilm so to save as many works as possible as quickly as possible. Then slowly, in the eternity that they had left, each book could be re-printed from these etchings as a readable text, one that you could see with your eyes and not a microscope. Miranda had been an apprentice when the last new book had come out—a collection of sonnets, *Astrophil and Stella*, in a language only she and a handful of others could understand. After that, right when they began the next transcription, the machine they used to read the tapes, the last of them, suddenly gave up the ghost. For seventy years they had been moving one by one through the hierarchy of texts, making each one readable and then casting them aside. Most of it was functional: physics, agriculture, engineering. Miranda read books on hydroponic farming and the construction of nuclear reactors, the basics of integrated circuits, the physics of fusion cores and warp gates. It was dazzling to see what once, eternities ago, the world had looked like, back when quantum physics still existed and people worked in factories and farming towers built up to the sky.

Life for Miranda meant repetition. There were enough wealthy people in the city to support a couple printing houses, mostly producing copies of old literary works that had made it through the sieve. There was of course still writing and still writers, but life was hard for them. Books were expensive, an enclave of snobbery, and nobody would be impressed by a library printed in the vernacular. So instead Miranda printed hundreds of texts in ancient languages that barely anyone could understand, since unreadable poetry in a dead language was what kept her stomach full, kept her living comfortably. Regularly she would check the orders that had come in, tell her apprentice what her tasks were for the day, and then go herself to the library to get the master copies they would work from. Then she and the apprentice would start, laying out and pressing copies of each page, folding and sewing them, and resting each set of finished pages in a box (the customer would buy the cover separately). Often Miranda stayed in late to finish just a few more pages, and to be alone with the feel and texture of the type. It was how she lived, over and over again, striking each blank day with the same design.

But on that particular morning things had fallen apart. The dawn that hung upon the stars and Gate woke swirled with storms and rain, tearing from their fixture the two small solar panels that used to live on the printshop roof. At daytime, when the panels would normally charge the batteries, they lay on the road letting nature go to waste. They only had a few candles in the building, which would not give enough light to work, and with the press in the basement there was not enough natural light to see by. The repair man they called said that, with the number that had been done to the wires, how the thatching on the roof had been all torn up, and you see here too the way the alignment's been thrown off so it's not like we can just put them straight on up again, and never mind the time it will take to charge the batteries up—well probably you're not going to be able to get the lights on again until tomorrow morning at best.

"Sorry, ma'am."

"It's not your fault," said Miranda. "I suppose there's some work that I could do at the library."

So she went and got the orders from her office and told the apprentice to keep an eye on the place for the day, and then went up the hill to the archive with a full day left and a morning's worth of work to do. With how hard it was to make type, the printing shops had all specialized by language and writing system, Miranda's shop taking care of several Romance and Germanic languages. Printing apprenticeships were famously difficult, stressing not only mastery of the technical aspects of setting type but also learning to read the languages used in the shop. Denova, the vernacular language used by much of the planet, started as a pidgin of English, Mandarin, and Arabic, with loan words picked up here and there like lucky charms (from French, Japanese, Cree, and quite a bit of Esperanto), until it emerged from the cultural pottage of the journey from Earth. Tonal, with about twenty phonemes, flattened vowels, and written right-to-left in a hybrid script, it was something of a masterpiece, practically designed to make learning the old languages as difficult as possible. But Miranda had shown a knack for tongues, delighting in their vagrant changes, the way an error in one time could be brilliance in the next.

As a child Miranda learned that she had been born in a strange time. The cyclical famines had mostly settled down and the population was stable. With so few major cities left, plagues and epidemics became less of an issue. For the first time in generations, people could imagine a future farther off than the next harvest. It was like the world had put on glasses. And with their sight corrected they could tell that they were standing at the edge of a cliff.

★

The library took up the top several floors of what had once been the central headquarters of the occupation. With the offices all hollowed out and the walls torn down, the old building, once a ship, held at least two copies of every book they managed to save from the nanofilms, in addition to the films themselves. Gadget had taken its name from this building, had been thrown up around it like a messy room, and even after all this time from the window of a study cubicle you could see out beyond the city the overgrown ruins of its abandoned districts, the beaten-up dirt roads that a hundred years ago were paved. Beyond them, squat in the distance like silhouetted dwarves, were windmills dancing in the breeze. On Earth, perhaps, outside the walls there would be a forest. Miranda would have liked to see a forest at least once in her life. But for the most part the tallest any plant could grow on Denovo was two, two and a half meters, not that much more than a person. Far out from the city, where the terraforming had gone farther, there was the black soil region, where at one time there had been an arboretum where wealthy Earthlings had gone to stroll among the elms and pines. But now it was all farms. You didn't want to let the soil go to waste.

It was lucky, it turned out, that the print shop had to close that day. By lunch time Miranda had finished all but one of the orders. Flashing her printmaster's ID at the door so the librarian would let her into the stacks, she chose a reading room and picked out each master copy she would need. The books were huge folios, containing multiple works in small text on the thinnest paper available. Back then, the job was too frantic to read the texts, to organize them by topic or author, so you would pull out a volume looking for a technical manual and find it between a math textbook and a collection of Japanese Rakugo tales. There were protocols for how to replace these master copies once they started to degrade, but the librarians wanted to put that off for as long as possible to avoid passing on some printer's new mistakes. So instead all the printmasters, over the length of a career, learned how to search through the numbered volumes, read efficiently and hone in on the work they needed, sketching out an index in their heads, a map of their small corner of the unforgotten world.

Yet sometimes even Miranda, experienced as she was, could get lost. Someone had placed a special order for some rare text, a novel called *Foundation*, which Miranda was almost certain had never reached print. But sometimes you'd get sent on fishing expeditions—from an idler maybe who had seen a book mentioned somewhere else and decided to place an order on the off chance that it still existed. And maybe it did. They had, after all, saved quite a few books, more than any person could read, or even keep track of. And the process had been too hasty to be rational. Certainly in the archive there were many books that had been saved and then forgotten, lost in yet another sieve.

With just the title to go by, she spent the rest of the day chasing after paper ghosts. She didn't even have the author's name. A living rumour, whoever it was survived in the dust that floated off book spines and thumbprints in the margin of a page. The rot and metal fatigue in the nanofiches had been unfixable for decades, and would be unfixed for centuries more. No one would ever read those tapes again. The book was gone and that was it. Not even a memory—just an offhand mention in some other work, a suggestion of what might have been.

However, unlikely things can sometimes happen. In fact, they happen all the time. And in that spirit, on the last dregs of the day, Miranda pulled a dusty, unread volume from a shelf and held it open, holding out the light to find a shade. Text in Arabic, a grammar of Hittite, what looked to her like Korean (though she couldn't read it), lists of equations and figures, musical scores, a treatise on the production of graphene foam—et cetera, etc, &c. All things that could have been interesting to another person in another time. It was always the scientific manuals and guides that frustrated Miranda, though of course she read them as they were printed just like everything else. They always assumed that you just had a bunch of helium-3 lying around, or a space elevator that still worked, or functional roads and sewer systems outside the largest towns. Or petroleum. It was as if the authors thought that just by knowing what a qubit was you could make a computer from scratch—just bootstrap yourself into the future. Easy. Who would ever have trouble with this? Just open a copy of *Baby's First Tokamak Generator* and work your way up from there.

Earth was lucky—it had oil, coal, trees, plenty of stopgaps on the way to nuclear fusion and all the power they would ever need. If they had used those resources up before they reached something sustainable, then they would have been in a lot of trouble. But Denovo never had that opportunity. A lifeless rock, without even an atmosphere, there had never been fossil fuels on Denovo because there had never been fossils. Its only resources were the stones and metals seeded into it by dying stars, heavy elemental dust cast off by supernovae and swallowed passively by gravity as thought caught up in the sieve-mouth of a giant whale.

Which explained the contents of the manifest that Miranda found in the obscure pages of that book—a list, in English, of every object on the ship when it launched the colonists from Earth, supplies to carry them for generations and then help them settle on a fateless rock. A section labeled "Hazardous Materials" caught her eye, and she skimmed down to find the prime offender: hundreds of tonnes of enriched uranium, enough to power a ship, a colony, a whole society cut off from its origin, terraform a planet, and then set up something more permanent. Miranda copied the numbers into her notebook and then went home to confer among her books. She had long ago read the proposed timeline for terraforming the planet and had seen how early it had been cut off—in the cruel window where the world would permit humanity to live but not to thrive. It was for this last, unmade push that the nuclear fuel had been meant for, the power needed for the ship and for the early stages of colonization being trivial in comparison. Once they reached the Asimov system, the solar panels could handle much of the day-to-day power anyway, and the reactors in the ship had been the most efficient on the planet at the time. With a little math and research, Miranda became convinced—most of the uranium was still there, and still useful. Hundreds of years of the stuff, enough to build up factories and farms, to build simple tools that made complex tools possible. In a century, perhaps, they could start work on a fusion reactor. And before that, radio telescopes and receivers: they could send a message back to Earth, use the warp gate to recalibrate the ansible, learn at last what happened more than a century ago.

Miranda knew that she would never live to see it all, the future that was out there, waiting, distant as the stars. But she could start them toward it, have at least the first dance if not the last. All she had to do was step out from the wall and ask.

★

Starlovers, the people living on the outskirts of Gadget often missed the beauty of the sky, which in the golden age had stayed hidden behind the glare of city lights. Only the pulsing iris of the Tannhauser Gate and the Clarke constellation (except for dim old Sol) were bright enough to break out through the sheen. But the gate, for most of them, was beauty enough. Its red lashes of plasma around a central lightless pupil day and night illuminating the intricate, colossal mechanism, while a persistent flow of small black dots, the numerous transport ships that travelled to and from the Earth, transited the glow, the second brightest star in the sky, a ruby brooch upon the Milky Way. And though the pupil was lightless, to stare into it was to glimpse the deepest outskirts of the future, to see into an eternity of human existence, the species stretching its legs out across the galaxy as though it were a bed. Or so the story went. Farther out from the city, in rural lands without bright lights, you could sometimes also see the lidded husk of a smaller portal, barely big enough for a single ship—the first gate, now decommissioned, which the Denovans had built themselves and through which the first people born on Earth visited this world at last. The portal through which they built their crimson star.

And then one day, without any fuss, the star went out.

That was all long before Miranda was born. And of course there were theories, arguments, long debates as to why and how the Earth had been cut off from them. It was all so academic, like the significance of the names the Earthlings had given the planet—first Asimov-c, then Planet Seldon, as if those words meant anything to the people living there. The *ESS Romulus* they insisted, to the very last, on calling the ship, seeming to take offence when you used the name the founders had given. The engineers and soldiers and politicians who came from Earth through the portal, who became the planet's ruling class, refused to learn Denova, and the rumour was they had sworn to their masters that they would never study it, and that neither would they fraternise with the locals, or teach them more about the Earth than they strictly had to know. And even if you befriended one, and convinced them to share, most of them could only stay for a few years at a time. Then their replacements, fresh from Earth, would respond to kindness from the natives with hostility.

In a sense, all this was ancient history. Miranda had learned it secondhand, first from people who lived through it and then from books, records, notes. And yet it was firsthand that she felt the past, her present once removed. Like how the council that ruled what had now dwindled to a city state, a backwater without a frontwater, sat in the same meeting room as the old politicians, kept records according to the same systems, still published new laws in ten Earth languages but not Denova. She knew firsthand how sometimes in the summer evening when the sun and Gate aligned just so, you could see reflected a vermillion swirl that must have been the hue that filled the eye when ships passed through all those many years ago. And firsthand she saw, if only in pieces, the old functions of the ship, buried now almost to the top, around which the whole town, the first town, had long ago been built. Earth, the old ruling class, it was all her present. It cluttered up her mind just as the dirt and dust clogged up her pores, just as the sandy wind filled up her mouth when she yawned.

It occurred to her that she had no idea what to do next. Drag the uranium up herself and then immediately die from radiation poisoning? It was highly enriched, and with its long half-life would be just as potent even after centuries. And then what would happen if she did bring it up?

Obviously she would need help, not only to bring the material to the surface but also to make use of it. She asked for an appointment to see the mayor, and after some berating got one on an early morning. Miranda walked in with all her notes and papers in a bag, with a map she drew of the bowels of the ship, where nobody had been allowed to go for years. What was it that she was proposing exactly? She was both aware and not.

"Are you Miranda?" asked the mayor, a tall woman, about eighty, and the third in her immediate family to hold the job. Indeed, most of the top political jobs in Gadget belonged to members of her family, held together more by necessity than love.

"Yes, I am." Miranda stepped through the door quickly, offering a handshake. "It is nice to meet you." The handshake was accepted. "I have a proposal here that I think you will be interested in."

"Indeed, indeed, my secretary told me. You say you found something in the archives?"

"A manifest of the ship, during the voyage here."

"Of course, there must be untold treasures underneath— technology we can't use, food and medicine long rotted, books that turn to dust as soon you touch them. Why are you wasting my time?"

"I have found something that will not be rotten. Indeed, something that, I think, will make you rather rich." That was how it would have to go, correct? No way she would let Miranda at this treasure without using it to help herself.

"You may not be aware of this, but I am already quite rich. Too rich to spend time on trivial fancies."

"Relative to everyone else today, yes you are. But compared to what your family had before the collapse I imagine you are not doing so well."

"That can hardly be helped."

"What if I know how to help it?"

"How?"

"Deep in the ship, near the very bottom, far below even the old fusion reactor, in a part of the vessel I don't think the old engineers ever modified, there's a treasure from the journey here. Uranium, meant to power the terraforming project—most of it unused. I have gone over the manifest and I have done the math. There is enough down there to give us power for centuries."

"Hmm." She leaned back to think for a moment. "You know we struck uranium at the edge of our territory maybe thirty years ago. We tried to get a reactor up but could never make it go."

"It wasn't refined enough. Back on Earth they would use these giant centrifuges to separate out the impurities before they did anything with it—otherwise the reactor won't work. But we can't build those centrifuges because we don't have the power, and we can't get the power because we don't have pure enough uranium, or a working fusion reactor, or oil, or coal, or you get the idea."

"And the uranium down below is different?"

"It's about as pure as you can make it. Someone could detonate a bomb with this stuff."

"Hmm." She drifted into thought again. "You know— Miranda, was it?"

"Yes."

"Why the founders called this ship the Gadget?"

"I've heard stories."

"And I've heard facts. Back ages ago, in the twentieth century, when the Americans invented the atomic bomb, The Gadget is what they called their first prototype. The one they blew up in an empty desert so that when they dropped it on people, they could be sure that those people would die. I wonder if the colonists, hearing that they carried tonnes and tonnes of weapons-grade uranium, gave their ship that nickname as some kind of joke."

"That had never occurred to me."

"Whatever. We don't even know if it's still there."

"But if it is, we could reverse the whole decline. Think of all the people we'd help."

"There's no way the engineers would just leave something that valuable just sitting there. And we can't really spare anyone to go check."

"You have nobody able to do it?"

"Right—go down into the most dangerous part of the ship and look for the rocks that give you cancer. Who would accept that kind of suicide mission? You?"

"I—"

"Well?"

"I, uh, I guess I have no choice."

"I'm not willing to spare anyone else. You'll get rations, a radiation suit, and a Geiger counter. Maybe some rope. Now get out of my office. I've got another meeting."

★

Ariel had known that this was a very bad idea, and had told Miranda, who agreed. A woman had come to their workshop the next morning to deliver the supplies, to show her how to put on the suit and read the sensor, to inform her that even with the suit if she got too close to the uranium she was as good as dead, and to make sure she signed a form that said that this mission was her idea and taken under her initiative. Ariel had followed Miranda to the entrance to the basement, a deep shaft that had once been an elevator, and had watched them toss a rope ladder down for Miranda to use "in case she needs to get back up." To think, a fifty-year-old woman, a skilled artisan, climbing down an elevator shaft on a rope ladder wearing a radiation suit, looking up at all the bewildered faces, the last human contact she would ever have. What a useless ending. After eight days they declared her dead.

But if it had been possible to talk Miranda out of her plan then it would have given Ariel one less thing about her to love. She was always obsessed, and wonderfully so. Not so much with the power plants and electricity, the factories producing advanced fertilizers and medical supplies, the electric train lines running up and down the planet like dewdrops on an apple's skin. Those were wonderful ideas, vital even, but for her they'd only been a means to an end. Ever since she started her apprenticeship, Ariel had had something of a crush on

Miranda—watching her focus as she set type, the way the world would vanish around her, the way her hands seemed to be in seven places at once as the finished page assembled from the air. But more than that, it was the way that she would talk about the books she printed. If you asked her, she would tell you that nothing was more painful than reading about science, since almost all of it was out of reach—practically, if not theoretically, impossible. Ariel, nevertheless, remembered walking in on Miranda reading, with a smile on her face big enough to eat her head. Ariel asked her what it was.

"Oh," said Miranda, "just a history book. About particle physics. *The Standard Model and After.* There's this wonderful— I mean literally, literally wonderful—description about this neutrino detector they built on Earth around the start of the twenty-first century. You've read about neutrinos, right?"

"Not really."

"They're these sub-atomic particles, so small they can just whiz right through you, millions of them, without touching you once. They are to atoms what atoms are to us."

"How do you even detect those then?"

"Oh it's clever, so brilliant and clever. Like measuring a planet with a wooden stick. Because you see it took them until the twenty-*second* century to really pin down the physics on how the particle interactions worked, and after that they could just make any passing neutrino interact with the sensor no problem. And that's too easy, and boring to read about. What they had to do before that though, was they dug underground these huge tanks of water and lined it with sensors, and then they would wait for the one in, oh I don't know, one in some huge number chance of a neutrino hitting a water molecule, which would release a bit of energy. And that energy is what they would detect. That's just so. *neat.* Like that story I told you about Cavendish weighing the Earth in his garden shed."

"It's very clever."

"Yes it is. And it just shows you—if something is there you can find it. You can't exist without leaving a trace behind, a shiver in the stardust. People just need to do the work to find it."

With that same tone she had told Ariel about the uranium cache, had shown her the route she'd plotted through the underbelly of the ship, even had Ariel make a copy of the map for safe keeping. And Ariel wondered—was she thinking of her neutrino detector buried deep under the ground? The great effort it would take, the kind that demanded a huge, complex society, one where people weren't just one bad year away from famine—what she'd enable if she found it. And both of them knew it. What stood between Denovo and the world of Minerva's science books were the same things as always: energy and food. And if you had the first one, the second became a lot easier.

And what else could everyone do, if they had all that? What would people do if you gave them a future? A life of had work, anxiety, the looming promise of a world growing steadily worse: one made, actively, more terrible by people and forces more powerful than you could even understand—it was a kind of poverty, to be futureless. And it leadened the mind as much as any other. But when Miranda realized what she'd found, the weights fell off, had dropped out from her ears and rolled out on the ground. The choice then, as she said she saw it, was to risk her life in the underbelly of the ship, or put the weights back in. So down she went. And she did not come back.

But she had left a map. At least.

Once they declared Miranda dead people began to talk, people in the printers' guild. Ariel was about eighteen, already skilled at her trade, had already passed the language tests. Why not let her graduate early—just a little early, to be frank—given the unusual circumstances and the loss of a skilled master. There was already a shortage, and now a perfectly good printing house was sitting idle, with unfilled orders in the storeroom just rotting away. It seemed like the logical thing to do.

And perhaps that would be a future, or at least something like a future. Yet the betrayal twisted her intestines. It stole her sleep. What had she been doing when Miranda died? Was she asleep? Or eating? Working? Playing? Had she for just an idle instant forgotten her worries, let her head fall back in a laugh, while her master, scared and lonely, breathed her last into the dark?

So sure, she said, she would accept the promotion and take over Miranda's shop. That would shut them up at least and keep people busy while they prepared the ceremony, called her parents over from their village, wrote speeches—lying speeches—about how Ariel would do well as Miranda's replacement. As though Miranda could have a replacement.

While this was happening, Ariel read over the map and gathered her supplies, exercised, and wrote a will. On the tenth day after her master left, she snuck off to the elevator shaft, waited for the guards to change, and hastily climbed down. Perhaps out of respect, or maybe wishful thinking, they had not pulled the rope bridge up. Good for them.

★

Why had she waited so long? Ten days. Miranda had rations to last that long, but did she bring enough water? According to the mayor's office, they had no real sense of which parts of the system had been deactivated when they closed off that part of the ship, so it was possible she could find running water in the sinks, showers, toilets, which she would have to disinfect of course but which would supplement what she had brought. Because of the damage that had been done, they had no idea what routes would be closed off, what doors would be jammed, and so could not really estimate how long the journey to the bottom would be. They gave Miranda a marker with phosphorescent ink that would let her sketch her path in glowing yellow lines so she could find her way home.

In the dim shadows of the underbelly, Ariel saw the first mark. An X, complete with serifs, just the kind of thing Miranda would draw. She saw in the distance the glow of a second one and went towards it, following them step by step. The distance between them was irregular, growing closer in curving hallways and farther on straightaways—probably, Ariel figured, so that on her way back Miranda would never have less than two markings in her sight at a time. It was convenient for Ariel too—though for the first leg of the trip Miranda followed, more or less, the route she had planned, Ariel knew that at some point, *something* had to have gone wrong.

Even after all this time, all these generations, it felt transgressive just to be inside. At the height of Earth's control of Denovo access to the ship was restricted to only Earthlings and their most trusted aides. Almost none of the natives were allowed in, and even then, the bottom section of the ship was strictly limited to Earthling engineers and army personnel. It was where they kept the fusion reactor, which produced power for the entire planet. Though Ariel hadn't spent as much time studying the physics as Miranda had, she knew that the reactor was an extremely complex machine, so large and so intricate that no one person, no twenty people even, knew enough to explain how it worked. Back when the Gate still worked, no one outside the engineering team was allowed to learn either about the reactor itself or about the advanced physics it involved more generally, and neither its fuel nor its replacement parts could be manufactured on Denovo. The reactor was not the only technology that came with rules like these, which applied to things like the warp gate, the high density farms, but they were enforced most strictly with fusion. Earth knew that so long as Denovo depended on them for their energy and food, there would never be either rebellion or revolt. Yet despite it all, the people could just look up—look at the sky for just an instant—and see a trillion fusion reactors, all running at full capacity, all to decorate their eyes and lift them from the soil and their work.

Earth had learned its lesson from Mars and Venus, the two colonies it had started before they sent ships beyond their star. The Martian terraforming had been the most difficult, since the planet didn't have an electromagnetic field to protect it from the sun's radiation. Instead what they did was build a space station at the Marian L1, the Lagrange point between the planet and the sun where the two gravitational fields exactly cancelled each other out. The cone of protected space that the Euler Station provided made Mars the first completely self-sufficient Earth colony, and its success prompted the Venus mission, the trip to what was then called Asimov-c, and a ship they sent to the

Trappist system that they never heard from again. And it was this success, too, that spurred Mars to assert its independence, to refuse to be a home to only tax evaders and mining companies and their indentured workers, a place for Earth's governments to test-run new policies before they used them on themselves. The rebellion had no chance at success, in part because the Euler Station was such an easy weakness to attack, but the attempt terrified the Earth, which began to clamp down on the colonies and slow the terraforming of Venus, which by this point had gone too far to stop.

It was around this time that they received Denovo's transmission, which said that they had completed work on the small warp gate they had built, and asked to begin synchronization. Warp gate technology was still a long ways off when the Gadget first launched, but in the centuries that the people on that ship traversed the blackened sky, technology on Earth advanced, and when the time seemed right, they sent a message to their colonies, offering a chance to reconnect. By cutting a path through a wormhole, the gates provided what was in all practical terms teleportation, but they could only work if there was already a gate at both ends. So you couldn't send yourself to a place you had never been, but if you just so happened to know of a functioning society in the far-off reaches of space who might be willing to help—well, now you were in business. Realizing the opportunity, Earth sent messages out towards its near-forgotten colony ships, explaining how to build the gates. Only one world answered back.

Nobody knew why that was, or whether the Trappist ship was the lucky one. Theoretically, if managed right, those ships could support a population for thousands of years, and there was nothing to stop the crew from just firing their engines in a random direction and letting themselves drift forever in the black. It would be almost nice, thought Ariel, staring down a hallway dark as the middle of a warp gate's eye. Total freedom, rootlessness, living off the gifts the past had given you. Drinking deep the dregs you stole. Or maybe they all died—from a radiation leak, from rebellion, from disease. Maybe a rock hit them;

nobody knows. Thousands of people, all that work, millions of frozen embryos in artificial wombs waiting to populate the new world.

But bless the untouched Trappist worlds, allowed to be uninhabitable in peace. Blighted deathworlds, gorgeous pearls of storms and dust, much like Denovo had once been, much like the first emissions of a star. The Earthlings never got to you— never snuffed you out.

★

Two days of walking and Ariel had begun to wonder at Miranda's thoughts, her dauntless constancy. Perhaps this is what happens when you send a printmaster into a cave with nothing but their wits and a magic marker. The spacing of her marks, the specificity of the X, the evenness of the lines, it all stayed constant even after days. Ariel had stumbled over one of Miranda's old campsites and found that the dust had been swept, the wrappers from the ration packs lain neatly in a pile.

Ariel began to worry. She had of course seen Miranda in the past reach these heights of obscene conscientiousness. It was always when she was most stressed or most afraid. It was her way, Ariel assumed, of seizing control of the situation: sure, she was lost in a dark tunnel deep underground looking for a cache of weapons-grade uranium, *but at least this X can be the very best X ever drawn by human hands, God dammit.*

She had plenty of reasons to be stressed. Early on, a caved-in hallway had diverted her completely off-course. She had the same old map that Ariel did, and so it was possible to predict how she re-routed. But that map was based on when the facility was new and functional. Ariel ran her finger up and down the slender hallways, the room labels all written in English. So many of these places didn't exist anymore. That map, half fiction and half fact, could be more dangerous than having no map at all.

Miranda was also consuming her rations too fast, if the discarded wrappers were any indication. They were calorie-dense, vitamin-rich, each a meal on its own yet only as big as a candy bar. Miranda should have only been eating about two of them per day, yet she seemed to have been eating four.

Ariel remembered as a child eating this stuff. Her father worked on a farm far out from the city centers, near a village on the edge of the civilized parts of the world. With the soil quality so poor, it took a vast expanse of land to grow enough food to feed a village, and so distant from the city it was impossible to get machines to plough and seed the land with. So they would work for days on end, with their hands and the backs of animals, living off these ration packs and plopping down to sleep on the dirt that fed them. Whole troupes of people, her family mostly, would over two or three days take care of the entire field, sleeping together in a circle, an eight hour walk from home, far too exhausted to appreciate the sky.

It had been ten years ago, when she came to Gadget with her father to ask about maybe this year finally getting a tractor, that Miranda saw her, heard the dulled intelligence behind her voice, offered to help her father buy his tractor—provided that he give her something in return. It was an odd way to find a vocation, but Ariel took it. Miranda had said that Ariel could visit her family any time she wanted, wouldn't even have to worry about paying for the trip, and two or three times in ten years she had taken up the offer. But she was happy, really, to live too far away for easy visiting. And the ration packs she ate, despite their sweetness, had the feel of soil in her mouth.

Leaving that village had been a second birth. And going back home felt like trying to crawl back in the womb. Was that the feeling she had now, the deep uneasiness, which gave Miranda so much stress? The transgression of the origin, and the rejection of the new beginning—the gift the future always takes up from the past?

Without thinking, Ariel unwrapped her third ration bar of the day and started to eat.

The pathway through the Gadget was growing more improvised. As the second day bled into the third Ariel followed Miranda's glow over boulders of crushed concrete and through a ventilation shaft. She found a window she believed Miranda had smashed herself, since the pieces had fallen on the opposite side as all the other broken glass—towards the centre of the ship and not away. She tripped over skeletons, avoided sparks from severed wires. Where did their power come from? Had they not completely cut off this part of the ship when they abandoned it? Had the depths of the Gadget been siphoning electricity from the windmills on the surface, powering for all this time sparks and lights that no human ever saw? Halfway through day three, Miranda's hand developed a tremor. Ariel walked by a mess of failed markings where Miranda had struggled to draw a straight line and failed. She seemed to have given up thereafter, writing quivered squiggles where her letters had once been. Had it pained her much, to lose a comforting obsession? Nothing yet remained to say.

Corpses became more numerous as Ariel approached the core, what was left of the team they'd sent to manage the disaster. It was still a matter of debate what the engineers had been planning to achieve, but the theory most people believed was that, cut off from Earth, they had tried to do maintenance on the fusion reactor with improvised parts. This plan had gone about as badly as anyone would have expected, and the explosion left the base section of the ship irradiated for decades.

With the power cut off and infrastructure crumbling, and with most of the old ruling class now dead or dying from radiation poisoning, the food riots quickly turned into a revolt. The people who stormed the Gadget back then and held the surviving engineers and generals at gunpoint probably thought they were staging a revolution. But it was not until they got a hold of the planet's Governor and, through a translator, interrogated him that they understood the depth of the problem. The planet was, as the Governor had said, "maximally fucked." His bluntness saved him: not knowing how to handle a global systems collapse, the revolutionaries let him take charge of the transition, the preservation of texts, the construction of the new government.

Though barely related to him, the mayor of Gadget was among his descendants. When society crumbled and with wolves skulking at everyone's door, it was the already-rich, the inheritors of the old colonial power, who made it through the bottleneck with the fewest losses. Now these princelets fetishized a lost decrepit culture that had no love for them—but which resembled power, the only warmth that still remained inside their chasmed hearts. When the guild was first founded, new printmasters had to swear an oath that said they'd preserve what was left of the Earth's great fortunes. Instead now they all got wealthy selling poems to the illiterate rich. Remembering her paymasters made the darkness seem less dreadful. Ariel trekked on. Perhaps, if she survived, she would translate some of those old works into Denova and send copies home to her parents.

As Ariel picked through the dense, macabre detritus of the old regime, she saw in the distance a set of broken windows and a door torn off its hinges beside a glowing mark. She stepped over the debris, put her head trough the door and looked around. And through that door a universe was opened up to her: a toroid monument, regal even in decay, stretching up so distant and so high that it seemed like it would swallow up the moon. The fusion reactor, blasted black and crumbling, insides melted by its own abundance, still from its sheer scale appeared enough to call a planet into being. Energy for an entire society had started in this place, this spot upon which Ariel now stood, where days ago she knew Miranda had stood, this place that in lost ages held the outline of a star. Now ripped and blasted in its dying throes, the void of an iris which was all that was remaining of its supernova pulled Ariel along with its enchanting darkness towards the deadly metal radiating from its womb.

Compressing hydrogen to helium, through to iron, in their death throes vomiting the denser elements, the stars had mothered every atom in the universe, just as their energy filled the bellies of all life on every planet everywhere. Even the neutrinos, those subatomic ghosts, began as fire in their breath. Ariel felt the spectacle overwhelm her. Her senses could not cope. So for an hour—just an hour she could spare—she sat and stared into the dark and pregnant nothing of the room, feeling herself growing separate from her self, she forgot for just a moment even who she was.

★

It was clever what they'd called this place, thought Ariel. "The Prospero Reactor," like the English word "prosperity." Perhaps that was the word for what this place had brought— prosperity, of a certain kind, for certain people, anyway.

The tapping of her boots against the metal steps of the ladder echoed through the all that was the room.

The markings continued at the bottom. Miranda followed them, though the ground was slick and rough, like volcanic glass, and the darkness that crept beyond the beam of her flashlight felt like it was chasing her. Her footsteps echoed back—the walls were laughing.

Back when the light went out, when the Tannhauser Gate shut off so suddenly, without even the kindness of a supernova, that it took days, and sometimes years, for people to accept that the world had changed. There had been so much incessant chatter about origins and causes—*why* the gate had closed, *how* the gate had closed. Perhaps, Ariel wondered, people wanted so badly for it to turn back on that they searched for benign causes like mirage water on a sea of sand.

Hope was no longer on offer, and so people lost interest. But Ariel still wondered, and sometimes in her idle hours, maybe with a history book on her lap, she would piece together what she believed went on. He best guess was the Venusians. After the Mars disaster, their militia was the strongest, and they had wanted independence from Earth the most. In the years before the shutdown, there was chatter about the Earth trying to build a Dyson sphere, how its energy consumption had grown so great that even fusion reactors were having trouble keeping up.

The plan was to encase the sun over many generations, with Venus as the staging ground, and all the power sent back to enrich the Earth. The colonies had always been glorified strip-mines, resources deposits that happened to have people living on them, but once the Earth set on building the sphere the demands on all the colony worlds grew more intense. Venus, as the closest to the sun, got hit the worst. And soon, Ariel believed, their hatred of the Earth became unquenchable.

What exactly had happened? A surprise attack? Perhaps. Certainly, a good strategist would have hit the Earth side of the gate first—since it was to them what the Euler Station was to Mars, the main causeway to and from the other planets, and the only way that Earth could feed itself. Ariel, who liked to play the armchair commander, imagined how she would do it. With the convenience of the warp gates, nobody would expect you to send an armada from Venus directly, elastic-banding between gravity wells over months or years, disguised perhaps as asteroids. It was a terrible idea, which is why it would be a surprise. So the ships appear from behind the Earth's moon and blockade the planet—devastating! A planet that hungry couldn't last too long without its colonies to eat.

Capture the gate and shut it down, then dare them to attack you. Oh that must have felt so good, to be the admiral of that fleet, to stand on the bridge of your capital ship and give the speech that would end the world. They might strike back and they might win, but there would be no coming back from this. The Earth, cut off, would consume itself. They could shoot your ships but not your planet, never take back what they lost. The war was won before it had even been declared.

At least that's how Ariel imagined it, and perhaps she was close to the truth. But there could be any number of causes— maybe an asteroid had hit the gate, or perhaps there was an accident on board. But Ariel enjoyed her tale, her admiral, her speech. At least it meant that the end had come for reasons that made sense.

But of course, the world did not make sense. Though at least Miranda did. Ariel saw at the horizon of the dark a placemark curving downwards to a hole. The opening was small, and looked like it came from the explosion. Ariel looked down and saw another marking deep inside, in what must have been some kind of maintenance tunnel. She thought back to Miranda climb-ing down the rope ladder in her bulky radiation suit. The tunnel would have barely been wide enough for her. But she would have known that the only way to the uranium was down, deep below, and that the oppressive darkness of the ossified reactor could continue without end. She would have taken whatever out the world had offered her.

Ariel squeezed into the tunnel and followed it down. There must have been, back ages ago, a way to get the uranium in and out of its containment easily. The fusion reactor, for all its glory, was a retrofit. What had been there before? Perhaps a nuclear plant. But once the plant was gone, why not get rid of the uranium? Why build your city on a bomb?

Perhaps that was too simple. The uranium had, after all, survived for hundreds of years by the time Earth took over, so it must have been stored well. Why take the risk of moving it without good reason? Safer, easier, to leave it in place, where you know for a fact it's safe, and maybe pour some concrete over it to be extra sure. After all, it's not like they needed it—fission reactors had been obsolete for centuries. Since not long after the ship set off. Better instead to let it decay in peace.

Probably if the mayor was going to use this stuff, she would have to order an excavation—don't bother carting it up through these narrow passageways. Just dig in from outside. Yes, thought Ariel, that would probably be a better idea.

★

The tunnel lead to a hallway, which lead to more hallways, which lead to a funicular and a shaft that went on down and down. It was day four. Ariel felt the darkness gnaw at her. She missed the sound of humans talking. And she missed the sun.

A ladder, thankfully, went down the shaft, and at the bottom was a dead end.

But not a dead Miranda, which at this point is what Ariel expected to find. Fallen on her head, or starved, or having given up. The rescue mission had become a quest to retrieve the body, and maybe take back news of her success.

Yet at the bottom of the pit here was a wall of fallen debris, not at all far from where the map said the uranium should be. Here was the path and no way through it, and here was Miranda's mark without the woman or her corpse. At this point Ariel thought it possible that Miranda had just vanished, or that perhaps she had never existed at all. Would that not be funny? A real good laugh. Something to tell the kids about back home.

But no, the real answer was so much less amusing. When Ariel turned around she saw, folded neatly in a back corner, Miranda's radiation suit, with a big star drawn over it. Ariel could not imagine why Miranda would continue—would go *towards* the uranium—without her suit on. On a hunch, she turned back to the wall and, with greater care, shined her flashlight over it. And there was the hole, a tiny opening, held up by a steel bar used like a lever, barely large enough for a person to get through.

Miranda hadn't given up, even when faced with a solid wall. She had pried open a small passage big enough for her to get through, though it meant taking off the suit.

Ariel was younger, and in much better shape, so when she took a hold of the bar and pulled she managed to dislodge the wreckage farther, and made it wide enough for both her and the suit to get through. She put it on. Some dim lights in the hall were still active, and she could see the remnants of the building, perhaps the only part of the ship still like it was on the ancient journey to their world. The lines painted on the concrete—had those been painted on Earth? And had so mundane a thing come the long way to Denovo, waiting in the dim lights just to hold her mind in place? It was very possible.

As she continued down the tunnel, Ariel started to hear a faint and dreadful echo—the Geiger counter's clicks. They started faintly, very faintly, until she reached a large door made of lead and concrete, open very slightly ajar. Ariel pushed through and instantly the sound was louder. Just a few steps forward she found what she had sought.

The body of Miranda lay at the bottom of a deep hole. That pit, by rights, should have been twice as deep, but it had been filled with concrete long ago. Ariel saw the rope Mirada had used when she tried to climb down—to get a better reading, perhaps.

Or maybe, knowing that the end was near, she had wanted to die as close to her prize as she could get.

Ariel slid down the rope and clutched her master's corpse, hugging it tight, weeping into the mask of the suit. This had been what she'd expected, but that made it no better. It hurt no less for being logical. It hurt no less for being true. She wailed up into the darkness, and the darkness, mockingly, wailed back. Beside her foot the Geiger counter screamed. And above Miranda's head, in the yellow marker, were the words "I found it!" neat in steady letters scrawled.

She took a moment to regain her composure, to refuse for now to grieve, as much as she desired to. She tied the loose end of the rope around the body, climbed out of the pit, and hoisted it up. A fall had broken her legs, and beside where Miranda's body had been was a large pool of dried blood—what likely in the end had killed her. Yet her face as well was stained with radiation burns. And a doctor would probably find even more radiation damage in her skin and bones.

So that's how it would have to be: her dead body would stand as evidence that the uranium was real, the agony she suffered in her final hours being the inscription of its signature inside her tissues and her cells. And if Ariel hadn't gone after her—well, then her death would have been taken as a sign of failure. Indeed, it already had. But Ariel saved her that at least.

Slowly now, careful with her rations and her step, following the placemarks in their intended order, Ariel dragged the body back up with her to the surface. Trudging steadily, waiting till she saw the sun again to feel her grief, Ariel let nothing slow her down.

Or almost nothing. At the bottom of the ladder leading out of the old fusion reactor, Ariel for just a second turned to look back up and see again the infinity that was the dark. She stared into it and permitted the disaster of its stark perfection to etch itself into her eyes, as though she had been gazing deep at an eclipse. The vastness of its shadows loomed as bright and powerful as the light that had been there—the pulsing fire that propelled the cosmos and the world, the life that lit the sun and other stars.

## The Lights Won't Touch Our Faces

For the sake of the argument, let's just agree to set this story "once upon a time" and "in a land far, far away." If I've learned anything from my time under the eaves, is that you don't want to go and make trouble where trouble doesn't already exist. Let the world happen without you—live like you aren't even there. Else you might end up in the lamplight with the killers and the dead.

Not many people know much about the "theatres," what goes on inside. In far-off lands they call them "courtrooms," because that is where the members of the court all gather, hidden in the shadows, wearing masks of porcelain, their monster faces eagerly devouring the show. And then me in the front, under the penumbra, just where the lamplights and the shadows meet: a theatre critic, an open secret, with two fingers scratching my uncovered face—a signal to the accused.

I suppose this story will do: some years ago there began something of an avant-garde in the theatre world. It began, as all art tends to, with a bad idea. I was there as usual, watching the flow of the trial, attempting, with nothing but my eyes and my experience, to predict the result. As I learned during my apprenticeship, there are seven basic plots, three of which end with the accused peasant going free and four of which end with them hanged. The lawyers, masterful performers that they are, improvise within these bounds, each one taking the old structures, and sometimes plagiarizing whole scenes and monologues, and within them making wholly new productions out of pure collage. Indeed, despite the art's commitment to formulas, creativity among lawyers was highly prized. It is a long apprenticeship—working as a bailiff or a scribe to observe the scenes from within, with the most senior apprentices taking the part of the judge—but the result is the stuff of fantasy. Each attorney steps forward and becomes a different person. Just a change in posture, a wrinkle in their robe, a new vibration in the voice, and suddenly a scene you've watched a thousand times surprises you. Honestly, that's half the fun. A good lawyer can act so well you forget that the trial is real.

Aside from the lawyers and their apprentices, the only people who see enough shows to learn the patterns are the nobles, who sit spectating under the eaves, pretending to not exist. Their masks preserve their solemnity, or the simulation of solemnity, in recognition of the sacredness of the events. But beneath those masks—anguish, joy, anxiety, suspense. Though the talent lies with the attorneys and apprentices, the real show, the thing that has drawn the rich to these theatres for four and a half centuries, is the accused. Typically a peasant, but sometimes a merchant or an artisan who angered the wrong person, they stand accused of at least one serious crime, but often several more.

Indeed, these days it has become common for the prosecution and defence to coordinate the charges in advance so to create the best admixture of suspense. Murder is too cliché. Say instead he robbed a church collection plate to pay for a goat he planned to fuck. Say she set her enemy's house on fire while he lay sleeping inside and then pissed in the well by the hospital where he recovered. Say that the two of them stole a horse from the Duke's stables and rode it naked through the marketplace throwing rotten tomatoes at the guards and fondling each other in full view of everyone. I've overheard them planning, coughing out absurd crime sprees while they laugh and drink and strategize— the true crime, which itself may not have happened, now well and suitably forgotten.

A terrified accused, and some paid-off witnesses, all coached into following the lawyers' direction, and none of them familiar with the way the system works—of course their anxiety is immense. So sometimes they manage to pool their funds and hire a critic like me. It's not to help them get out of trouble, since often nobody knows in advance where the improvised trial will go, but to warn them of what the result will be. On good days, with uncreative lawyers, I can give them an hour, maybe two, to send a runner and pack their things, skipping town before the guards come to confiscate their goods, lest the family be doomed with the accused. I've seen people scurry off to forge wills and to prepare funerals, or to lay a trap for someone who escaped the noose. My job doesn't technically exist: by law I and all my friends are interlopers, commoners who snuck into the shadows by the edge—and long ago, in the years just after the trials had ceased to be real trials, this was actually the case. But let's not talk about that.

Anyway, as you might imagine, you can't be right all the time. Occasionally you get some new hotshot who thinks he invented the plot twist, who makes a move at random that nobody expects. Your average critic gets it right seven tenths of the time, but I've been able to pull nine. You see, I figured something out, something that only me, the nobles, and the best lawyers in the kingdom have been able to see: there are not really seven plots. There is only one plot. And that plot is "screw the poor." Figure that principle out, and you will never be surprised again. Usually.

I suppose I should come clean about that avant-garde I mentioned earlier, the fancy new style that's come to town. It's something of a disaster, and it's partially my fault, part of that one-in-ten that I still haven't made go away. You see, the king for the longest time didn't go in for theatre like the other nobles, which was a problem for two reasons. First, because everyone likes what the king likes because the king likes it, and so things that the king doesn't care about tend to shrivel like a flower in the shade. But the theatre had survived indifference before. The second problem was more serious. The theatre was, in a legal and ceremonial sense, the delegation of the king. "The playhouse is the king's house," goes the saying, which is why common schlubs like me have to sneak in through the servants' entrance, and why the nobles still hide their faces, first in shadow then in gaudy masks, so no one can see them smile as they hang someone in the middle of the hall. Their presence too is trespass, of a certain kind. The whole pageantry of the event arises from the absent presence of the king—so if he doesn't give a shit, then what exactly are we doing?

There was an upstart lawyer, just the previous year given the title, who thought he had a solution. Among the upper classes there were those who did not appreciate the subtlety of the art, who did not see in the eternal repetitions of the plots an infinity of differences, those who could not be surprised if they knew how a story was about to end. The king, it pained us all to hear, was one of these sorts, a rube in taste if not in class. But, the young lawyer emphasized, the theatre's bad reputation was the result of hearsay rather than fact. The king had seen hardly any shows and had absorbed his opinion secondhand. So surely if they held a show, invited him as the guest of honour, and then dazzled him with the greatest performance they could muster— then, at last, he would see reason.

Someone called in a favour who called in a favour, and in a week the man in charge of the king's chamber pot began to casually mention all the fun the nobles were having at the theatre. That was enough at least to plant the idea, to get the king to pay attention when he overheard talk of the latest show, and to feign an interest when others brought the matter up. New to the throne, he had grown up cloistered, taught how to rule but not how to live. He would not admit that he believed that he was missing out, but he could agree to be convinced.

This stuff I heard about all after the fact, from a friend of mine, a minor lord who likes to go slumming with common people like myself. He was, as they say, a vintner, master of the grape vines, and so knew how to get his rumours fresh, even out of season. It was him, as well, who mentioned me when the young lawyer, who I would soon know as Harlequin, came asking about which critic had been hired for the crucial show. And it had indeed been me, for I was widely known to be the best. And the poor gentleman who was to play to part of the murderer had at least enough money to afford my services without pooling it from his friends.

Calling himself Inokori, he was the son of a merchant whose wealth he was set to inherit. But he blew his chances with a youth spent sleeping with the wrong people. A house of *nouveau riche*, their place below the eaves was always precarious, even with good behaviour. To protect the family's reputation, Inokori's father disinherited him, leaving him to scrape a living with petty tricks and scams. But, it turns out, the father always regretting the decision, and when he heard that his son had been plucked from the flophouse for the king's new show, had been given his lines and a charge of murder (and a few other things), that guilt metabolized into regret and soon he drew up plans to welcome Inokori to the fold again, should he survive. Now, of course, a clever merchant like Inokori's father knew what the cost would be in reputation if he announced that he forgave his son, or if he even acknowledged the man's existence and waited outside the playhouse for the news. He knew as well that justice was a lottery, and that Inokori's innocence meant nothing. There was no point in embarrassing himself for a son who was about to be hanged. The obvious solution was to hire a critic and have him signal the result to a messenger ahead of time. Looking through the secret window that everybody knew was there, the messenger would see in advance what the decision would be and then run it to the father. If Inokori was innocent, his father would come down to the playhouse to forgive Inokori in person, and if Inokori was guilty then the man would stay home to be alone with his grief.

There was a lot at stake—a wrong guess would have the man throw away his reputation for nothing, or leave him sitting at home while his vagabond son was thrown back onto the streets. So of course I got the job.

As for why Harlequin was asking about me—I had no idea. Critics technically do not exist, and the official word from the lawyers' guild was that allowing anyone other than the accused, the witnesses, the judge, and the attorneys to enter the house of the king was to verge on treason. But then again, the kings had tolerated our presence in their house for generations, and it wasn't as if people couldn't see us sitting on the shadow's welcome mat, the lamps of justice barely lighting up our faces. We did not wear masks.

It occurred to me that Harlequin had planned some kind of misdirection—that he was going to pay me off so that I gave the wrong kind of signal near the end, so everyone who knew to watch me (which was everybody in the room) would be surprised by the twist he pulled at the end. Over drinks with some colleagues, I mused aloud whether Harlequin could afford me, figuring my interest would get back to him somehow. But he never came around.

With my client paying all my travel fees it was a comfortable journey up to the capitol. To preserve the king's dignity, they would hold the trial in the Royal Theatre, which in addition to the usual trappings included a special box seat carved into the wall, with a shade hung over to preserve a darkness all its own. Aside from that the layout was unexceptional: a central pit, like a wooden doll's house, held desks and seats for all who were supposed to be there—two tables in the middle for the opposing legal teams, rows of seating in the back for witnesses, and a raised-up platform for the judge, a witness box. From the ceiling there were blazing lamps that lit up the central room until hardly any shadows could survive. The light was there to represent the allwatchfulness of justice and the eyes of the king. Recessed into the walls above was seating for the nobles, and to keep the darkness that they sought from leaking out all around their alcoves jutted eaves that cast thin shadows all around the floor's perimeter. That is where I was—on the floor against a wall beneath the eaves, barely out of sight and mind.

Just before the trial began, I slipped into the theatre through the servants' door and took my spot. The nobles, not wanting to miss out on the event of the season, had already taken their places in the dark. One or two of them for a moment met my eye and nodded recognition, one absent person to another. Their masks were all festooned—gaudy, decorated with bright colours and peacock feathers, smiling and frowning with great energy. I often wondered what their lives must be like, how much must rest on a sideways glance or a rumour of a frown, for their idea of a fun time to be an evening in a mask. Certainly it must give their faces a rest. Even with their expression covered, every quirk of decoration, I have come to understand, still had meaning—significance affixing to the porcelain like crust on a sleeping eye. There was a language of flowers and of fans, and now too a language of masks: who was in love, who was seeking out alliances, where each person stood in some infernal hierarchy. Whole dramas played out above my head in just the first few minutes as people filed in and scanned about for signals and for clues. Just imagine if they could see each others' faces, the burning havoc that would wreak.

After the lawyers and the judge and the accused all filed in, walked out to his seat King Pantalone and his attendants. Out of respect all stood at attention, save for the nobles and myself. Not really there, responding to his presence would be the height of disrespect. And though his seat held a private shadow, he also wore a mask—a plain one, flat and bearing no expression. He was a king without a face.

The judge, after conferring with his teacher, gavelled the scene to order. As was tradition, the accused Inokori stepped forward to the bar and prostrated himself out on his knees. As his council whispered in his ear he stuttered out:

"Your honour, most high and most merciful, I, Inokori, stand accused today of the crime of murder, theft, and fraud. It has been said that I accumulated an immense and unpayable debt while living at an inn in the city, taking advantage of their food and comfort for weeks without any intent to pay. I then lied to the owner, saying that I was being hunted by a gang of murderers, so that out of fear he would kick me to the street rather than insist that I work off the debt. When he and his employees refused to believe my lies, I came upon them in the night and cut their throats open with a knife I pilfered from the kitchen and then sold their bodies to a doctor to use in an anatomy lesson. It is up to the mechanism of the court to say whether or not these words are true, and out of respect to you, your honour, I enter no plea and will neither claim my innocence nor admit my guilt. It is with deep and humble gratitude that you pursue justice for me with all the wisdom you possess, in the name of the law and of the king."

Then Inokori stood up and returned to his seat. What followed was a parade of witnesses, each of whom rose and, prompted by the defense, presented their canned scripts. It was all well-choreographed, and moved according to tradition. The speech of the accused was like a prologue, establishing for the audience the general nature of the crime. Then the prosecution and defense would spar with each other over witnesses. It was in this section that much of the drama played out, the two sides like halves of a comedic double-act—the defense attorney as stooge, establishing the facts, putting up a wall off which the scene's infections energy could bounce, rebound, infuse the room, and amplify. And then the prosecution, that rabid genius Harlequin, was the comic relief, the driver of the scene. But though he drew the most attention, he could not work without his partner, any more than one could catch a ball that had never been thrown. Riffing off of the mistakes and lapses of the witnesses, setting each other up for wit and cleverness, letting the story weave and bend itself as it pleased from simple accidents, it was almost as if they had written out the scene in advance.

"Now for the benefit of the court," said the defense attorney, Columbina, "please explain to me your role at the establishment in question."

"I worked at the bar and sometimes as a waitress."

"And did you enjoy your work?"

"Quite a lot. It paid well. I made a lot in tips."

"Very good." Columbina walked up closer to the witness stand. "But you know, and this is just between you and me, I think you kind of got ripped off."

"How so?"

"Well you're aware I used to work in a restaurant."

"Really?"

"No. But I liked to pretend I did. And I have to say, without me there the whole place would have gone up in smoke—like it never existed! You ever feel that way?"

"They did have me close up every night, as if I had nowhere else to be. And sometimes the customers were a bit stingy, and rude when they got drunk."

"Exactly, exactly—you're the heart of the establishment, is what you are. So then," and here she turned to look at Harlequin, "*if* as you say you were the beating heart of the restaurant, working day and night to keep food in the pantry and wood in the stove, then *why*—*why* I ask you—were you not among the dozen or so important people allegedly murdered by my client on that faithful night?"

"I'm sorry, what are you saying?"

"What I'm saying is, your honour," she turned to the judge, "it may well be that we have accused the wrong person. My client is innocent: for if he is clever enough to pull off a trick like the one he's been accused of, and if he really sought revenge, then he is clever enough to know that the best way to destroy an inn is to kill the bartender. No, no, someone with a better motive has emerged. This woman here, angry after years of neglect, knowing full well her importance to the operation, murdered her superiors in the middle of the night and then pinned the crime on a quarrelsome customer. The pieces all fit together perfectly!"

"Your honour, I object!" said Harlequin.

"On what grounds?" said the judge.

"I happen to have it on good authority that the opposing council does not tip her waitresses. Clearly, then, she has internalized her guilt over stiffing, and I could go so far as to say *robbing blind*, the hard-working men and women of the city's inns and restaurants. So now she turns around and accuses an innocent waitress of enacting precisely the vengeance that she worries over every waking moment of her life."

"This is slander," said Columbina. "No waitress could ever sneak up on me like that. I happen to be a light sleeper. When I nod off, I float up to the ceiling. And anyway, just look at the witnesses, these scrawny arms of hers. I could totally beat her in a fight. There is nothing for me to fear."

The witness, with the fact of the accusation dawning on her, began to stutter a protest. But Harlequin spoke over her.

"You talk tough but I bet you couldn't lift a beer glass to your own mouth, much less fight someone off."

"Your honour, it seems I have no choice: in the name of justice, the king, and of my sterling reputation, I must challenge the opposing council to an arm-wrestling match!"

To be honest, I was getting rather annoyed with the production. It was all stock characters and stock phrases, and precious little improvisation. Meanwhile the witness, perhaps with visions of a noose around her head, began to sob quietly in the stand, the blood descending from her face as though she were already dead. Perhaps the lawyers were boring her too. Perhaps they believed that King Pantalone, being new to the theatre, would not yet be bored with the same old scenes and slapstick, that they could relax just as they would when performing to children. And perhaps that was true, but it felt like cheating. When one gets a chance to perform in front of the king, even if he isn't a connoisseur, you should still attempt to display your art to its fullest extent, to cut laziness away like fat from a leg of meat. Instead, these two gave a performance so sleepy and redone that it was impossible for me to tell what story they were aiming for. It was as though they were repeating ideas at random—there was no way for me to guess.

At least the bits were funny. Even if the humour wasn't exactly to my taste, you could always tell the jokes were landing when the nobles above were pretending not to pay attention. The jokes and foolery merely being an occasion for the witness's struggle, the real draw of the show. These witnesses getting brought to the theatre, who had only heard whispers about it, who maybe couldn't even see the audience, expected to be part of a serious proceeding of the machinery of justice. Watching the truth dawn on them as the events descended into farce—it was hilarious. Like a fly caught in an invisible web. And Harlequin, I could tell, was as talented as people had said. At points it was almost a struggle to keep my face on tight.

After a couple of hours, finally, there was a break. With the trial nearing its end, Harlequin made a gesture to the defence attorney, who pushed up Inokori to the witness stand. What began, I could tell from the first word, was what aficionados call the "Legrand," one of the several set-ups a lawyer might use to transition to the end—specifically a happy one. Yes, I could tell for sure at that point: Inokori was going to get off. I looked up to the king above, and from my angle, and maybe only from my angle, I could see his expression beneath the mask: happy, per- haps, and most certainly amused. What we had seen so far was not original, not new. Little more than a diversion for someone like myself, but to the untrained taste of the king it was quite gripping. In any case, no need to spoil the ending for him: I made my signal out the window discreetly, with the lift of a finger. Inokori's father would have plenty of time to reach the court- house, and would be waiting outside to greet his innocent son.

Harlequin began berating Inokori, drawing feeble apologies from him, grovels that began as tepid whimpers and then grew to grand productions of dishonour. Innocence would not be easy for him, and it would not be swift. The Legrand was kind in the end, but the lead-up was brutal.

"And what was it you called yourself, Mr. Inokori?"

"The one who makes—"

"Speak up so the king can hear you."

Inokori turned to face the king's platform, "I said I was the one—"

"Defendant, you will turn to face Mr. Harlequin this instant," shouted the judge over the banging of the gavel. "There is nothing behind you."

"But your honour," his hands were shaking like he'd come in from the cold, "the lawyer asked to make sure the king can hear."

"So speak louder. Project your voice. The king isn't behind you—any more than he's in front of you. His spirit is infused with the building, holding it together even more than the nails in the boards. The king resides in every corner of this room, and so you must ensure that every corner can hear you."

"Yes, your honour."

"Now answer the question."

"I call myself the one who makes a living my staying behind." He was almost shouting. Tears welled up in his eyes.

"And why do you call yourself that?" asked Harlequin.

"Well you see, uh, after I ended up on the streets—"

"And why were you on the streets?"

"Ah, yes, I was, um . . ." He paused for a moment, stuck. Clearly he didn't want to drag his father into this, but he also didn't want to lie.

"Oh you 'um' too much and now you're on the street?"

"No, I—"

"Is there a doctor you could go to? A therapist for people who 'um?'"

"I don't know, sir."

"It's what I tell apprentices all the time." I could see the judge nod along. "Don't 'um,' don't 'ah,' just speak the truth and speak it directly, as though the king were hovering above your shoulder. Because one day he might be!"

"I'm sorry, Mr. Harlequin."

"Are you sorry to me or are you sorry to the king?"

"Ah, I'm—um."

"What was that?"

"Nothing! I'm sorry to you *and* the king."

"Me and the king?"

"Yes."

"At the same time?"

"Yes."

"You ungrateful—your honour."

"Yes," the judge's face had gone stern.

"Please let the record show that I do not accept, and would likewise never condone such insolence as to apologise to a lawyer of this court and to the king at the same time. To even assume that we exist on such similar moral planes as to make an apology for me suitable for him, well, I don't want to accuse someone of blasphemy so quickly, but let it be known that my merciful heart has been tested on this day!"

Inokori at this point was seized by panic, utterly. "I didn't mean to imply—"

"Quiet now," the judge said. "You have said quite a bit more than too much. As for you, Mr. Harlequin, let the record show that the court is officially in awe of your munificence."

"Thank you." Harlequin paced knowingly towards the door, and then turned as though he were about to say something, when lightly, too lightly for anyone but me and him to hear, there was a knock. Heavily, Harlequin leaned himself against the door—as though the weight of justice itself were pulling him down. And then he turned again to questioning.

"Of course," Harlequin began, "we are all quite aware of why you call yourself 'the one who makes a living by staying behind.' There is almost no need to ask you. For it is well understood that you, for many years now, have been living on the streets and in the flophouses, using your silver tongue and noble bearing to talk your way into inns and brothels so to mollify the pain of vagrant life—'staying behind' as long as their kindness permits you to." He stepped closer to Inokori, on each word inching nearer, until he loomed above him on the witness stand, leaning with both hands against the bench. "Yes, we have seen already your facility with words, your cleverness, as you tried to talk your way out of perdition. Where, I ask, would such a lowly street bum acquire such a skill?"

"I'm not actually that good—"

"Don't flatter yourself. It's embarrassing."

"I suppose my father, um—"

"What was that?"

"I, I guess my father was the one—the person who, uh, showed me. The one who taught me how to speak."

"Your father?"

"Yes."

"He help you often?"

"Sometimes."

"What does that mean?"

"He used to help me a lot."

"And then?"

"He, uh, stopped."

"Why?"

"He never really said."

"I've heard enough." Harlequin stepped back from the bench and faced the judge. "Your honour, though it is my assignment on this day to prosecute Mr. Inokori for the murder, the higher principles of justice compel me to inform you that I believe that he is innocent of the crimes for which he stands accused."

A shiver went out beneath the eaves. For the first time that night Harlequin had diverted from the pattern. What should have happened, what was supposed to happen, was that after berating the accused the defense attorney would step in with some forgotten evidence, or a detail that had gone unnoticed, and unravel the prosecution's case from there. But Harlequin wasn't having it, and I had no idea of what he planned to do. Perhaps too quickly I turned to look out the window to the servant to see if I could stop him, but he was already gone. Glancing back, Harlequin had seen my desperation, and with daggers in his eyes he smiled.

"Who do you propose is guilty then?" said the judge.

"There is one person, I think, who could have done it—who had the means and had the motive. And luckily it appears this person has arrived."

Harlequin clapped his hands, and on that signal the door came open and two guards leading Inokori's father stepped inside. The light of the room spilled over his face and bore up his shock and confusion to the upper chambers of the room.

"What, I—I don't understand," the man turned to the guards. "I thought you two said the trial was over." He looked at me, his mouth hanging open, hate emanating from his eyes among the reflection of the lamplight. "What did you do?"

"Enough of this." A loud bellow. The king, delighting in his fury, had stepped up and leaned into the light. "The incredulity, the thoughtlessness—of a man, scarcely a noble, exposing his face in this sacred room and not even showing the barest evidence of respect."

"Your majesty, I—"

"No, the time for you talking is over. For I have already figured out how this scene ends. Even worse than disrupting the proceedings and dishonouring my presence here, it seems that to save your own reputation you cast your son onto the streets and then framed him for murder. Mr. Harlequin—is that your name?"

"Yes, your majesty."

"I hope I have not spoiled your plans."

"Not at all, your majesty. The gears of justice shall turn as intended."

"Good." The king, clearly enjoying himself, sat back down. "As punishment, I shall have my attendants strip this upstart family of their nobility—in addition to whatever penalty the court decides. Their money, I think, could build a new workhouse for the idle poor. Someplace for that wastrel son to live."

Harlequin bowed. The silence filled the room like water, and only he could swim in it. Not even the nobles knew what to do. The king himself, the actual, real king, had become part of the act. And it had all been Harlequin's plan—with my assistance, like a stagehand wearing black and moving props about, the audience pretending not to see.

The rest of the trial went as expected. Inokori's father, scorched by his dishonour, fell to his knees and accepted the fate that had been given to him. Hanged until dead from the roof of the courthouse and disposed of in a pauper's grave, not even his son would know where his body lay. Inokori, now, stood to inherit nothing, and had earned his now impoverished family's enmity. Last I heard he had turned to banditry on a road up in the countryside. No court of justice there: the body-guard of a travelling merchant one day put a sword between his ribs, and that was it.

In a way, for me, the failure had been formative. And when Harlequin's new trick caught on, and lawyers everywhere began to imitate, I was the best at spotting it. Always, when I knew a lawyer was trying to play me, I let them get away with it. To interrupt their plans would mean becoming too much a part of the show—and the shadow underneath the eaves had grown too thin already.

Finally, for a time the king began attending trials in his court, though only those where Harlequin presided. The lawyer had been too clever, it seemed, in realizing that the king would want to be drawn into the production—for he could not simply repeat himself, and he could think of nothing that would match the brilliance of his earlier success. Eventually, the king got bored with him, and soon after did everyone else.

Some years later, when I was near retirement, I saw him in a pub, tired and ragged and weeping quietly into his glass. The accoutrements of his success were old now, too long unreplaced they had begun to weigh him down. With nothing better to do that night, I took the seat across from him, and ordered us a round. After several quiet minutes drinking, I ventured to ask—

"Are you alright?"

And he replied, "I bet that you can guess the answer. I bet you know exactly how this kind of story ends."

And he was right.

## Lone and Level Sands

My ancestors painted the earth in greasy reds and whites, and my father raised our home on the cracking blue of his father's latter days. When I was a very small boy we dismantled that house, and I and my siblings carried it far to the east and set it down on the brown, uncovered earth. Soon, the soil was yellow in all directions, coming to a hard stop at the edge of a strip of pure black.

We were artists. The soil was our canvas, the sky was our patron, the birds were our critics, and the universe was our museum. There is, somewhere, an old historian who knows the whys and whens of our eternal masterpiece, who knows about the early days when the First People laid colour to the ground with brushes and buckets and mops. There are even a few who know what the painting will look like once it is complete one hundred years from now. I am not one of those people. Still but a boy, all day and night alone I paint.

We were all going to die. We had known this for a very long time, our doom—but we ignored it, bathing ourselves instead in the idle amusements and impossible fantasies of life after life had ceased to be. That could not last forever. When we, legion, awakened to our impermanence, life shut down immediately. We saw the feeble worthlessness of our creations. Our cities were but Babylons of stone and glass, our artwork but the scribbling of children, our families but the continuance of a blind chemical reaction. We did nothing, for nothing mattered.

Human beings are creative. We build and manufacture in bails and loads and tonnes, our artist dedicate their lives to the pen and the brush, our scientists surpass themselves in their discovery—but destruction is all that has true permanence. A statue built of stone, strong and elegant, will stand erect only until it crumbles. Once it is gone, it is gone forever. When the universe burns away, not even the rubble will survive.

How do we create meaning when all creation is impermanent? But that is the wrong question. For if we are the ones who grant meaning, then that meaning can never transcend us. We learned that our creation only needed last as long as we did. Once the last human perished, our work would again mean nothing, but by then it wouldn't matter. So we asked: "To what purpose should we dedicate our effort? For what creation should we exhaust ourselves completely?"

"Beauty," said my ancestor, voicing what they all believed. Beauty was the only real choice. And too it was a superior beauty, beauty etched upon destruction unlike any had ever seen. A scorched earth, scraped to canvas, its lifelessness foundation to the immortality of art.

The earth is now a very beautiful place, but only if you see it from high above. The land is flat, the trees are gone, the lone and level sands stretch far away. In the world is but one city and one factory, and that factory makes the food and paint and tools for all of us. The bucket I carry now is held not by me, but by the thousand hands of the city-dwellers, who build but do not paint. Others made the brush I use, and the long stick I wield it on. Just below the horizon, I can see a small puff of smoke. The flatterners are working ahead of us, in their great indominable machines. They never stop, and neither do we.

Orange was the colour of my childhood. Each day I would pack my kit and my rations and walk off to spread my daily paint. Each night I would return and wash the pigment from my face. My brothers and my sisters would do the same. I left bootprints in my creation as I came back. I used to worry about them, as I worried about the ridges and bumps of paint in my sloppy, childish work. My father told me that it did not matter, for nobody would notice. It was our role to make and not to see.

That house was the only constant in my life, as I moved from sector to sector and hue to hue. My parents died, my siblings died, but I still carried that house with me. In it was everything I owned and everything I created. My life covered the walls thick, like primer. It soaked the wood. I would leave behind all my effort, miles of paint applied with my own hands. But the house I would never leave behind. It was mine, even when the painting wasn't.

I grew old. I grew very old. One day, while I applied a light pink dye to what used to be a lake, I ran out of space. The next day I went looking for more soil to paint, but there was none. I sat in my house and waited for the next assignment.

There were very few humans left by now. The indoor farms of the city were poor substitutes for cornfields, and there were no doctors in the painted wastelands. I never met people any more. The radio sustained me. It buzzed one day, about a week after I ran out of room. I answered.

"Hello?"

"Hello, sector 24601?"

"Indeed."

"Have you filled your area?"

"Yes."

"Are you sure?"

"Yes."

"Ok, hold on." There was a rustling and an excited chatter. "Good, we should be getting back to you soon. Just sit tight."

"Alright."

It was about a two weeks before I spoke to a human again. It was a woman, a woman who came from the sky. She didn't come on a parachute like one of the monthly supply drops, but on a helicopter. She had my name on a list.

"24601?"

"Yes."

She shook my hand. "I have good news."

"Oh?"

"It's finished, the whole painting. The work is done."

They had been thinking for a very long time about what to do once the painting was complete. They decided that the best thing was to take everyone left alive up into space so that they could see it all at once. There was only so much room on the ship, so they were bringing people up a bit at a time. I was by then the oldest living human being, so I was going first.

Before I left, I asked them where they were going to hide my house. The roof needed a lot of work and I didn't want it staining the picture. They told me that it didn't matter. Everything was fine.

I climbed into the ship and it lifted off. Up, up, I saw my house and its ugly roof, I saw from above the little wood and plastic box where I stored my life for safe keeping. Up, up, now the house was just a little dot, the earth below was flat and uniform. Up, up, and then the dot was gone, but the painting was in view.

I saw the picture, a collage of intricate abstractions and patterned lines—what the designer though to be beauty given form. It was pretty ok. They let me stay up for a full day so I could watch a complete rotation. Yes, it was pretty alright. Then they sent me down again; it was someone else's turn. I went home and took a nap. When I woke up I wasn't sure what I should do. A long walk, some eating, a stare, emotionless, into the setting sun. I went to sleep again.

## CORPSE MENAGERIE

*Sometimes he overcame his weakness and sang during the time they were observing, for as long as he could keep it up, to show people how unjust their suspicions about him were. But that was little help. For then they just wondered among themselves about his skill at being able to eat even while singing.*

—Franz Kafka, "A Hunger Artist"

The pattern of Kay's death had been an accident. The artful plan of Wilco's flip and tumble from the parapet he'd copied from accounts of a retired master, as an apprentice painter learns their hands and noses in a gallery before later fashioning their own. Yet, of course, the true art of death was only for the patrons. Wilco, like Kay, his apprentice, and like every Corpse before him, could with but one exception see only the rehearsals, the preparation for the leap. Perhaps that is why, when the time was right, he failed.

The strings wrapped upon Wilco's hands tightened as, so high above the crowd their dark hats and open faces seemed to him like checker pieces on a grid, he flexed and unflexed his fingers nervously, his anxiousness encroaching on his thoughts. They were just strings that night, not razor-wires. Though, redded with dye, they would simulate the armature of the death, and the fulfillment of the plan. He stood high above the crowd and buildings, in an open area near the city's walls. The balcony, custom-built, and all the clockwork Wilco and Kay had put into it, was worth more than all the people in the audience made in a year. Its architecture, layered like the strata of the Earth, they could not have realized without the aid of their patron, the industrialist Carmillo Smith, though the days were long behind when a patron on their own could, or rather would, fund such a work entire.

Kay, her senses lit up with detail, had checked and double checked the gears on each outswinging arm. Like a great tree the balcony grew out, branches branching upon branches, each arm of arms articulating with its twin so to, it was intended, keep the wires taught. As Kay and Wilco built it up, section by section, they tested each new part on dead pigs they purchased from Kay's parents, who were butchers in the village where Wilco had found her. She had always like to watch her father and mother, both geniuses with knives, illustrate the sections of the pig, its different types of meat and viscera, with careful cuts. When Wilco, not yet bald and not yet wearing his signature plumb cape and golden tassels, came to her village in the mountains with the seedling form of his contraption, he did the same work in an instant when he dropped the body off a roof—the prototype arms and wires powered by the momentum of the falling pig.

The young Kay and her father, already late with an order, stopped for just a minute to witness the carving, and marvelled at the care of the arrangement, the specificity of each cut. Kay's father asked Wilco who his master was.

"Sigismund," Wilco said. "But I am a master now."

Her father seemed surprised. "That young man, the prodigy Sigismund? I only heard about his act a year ago, was hoping he'd come nearby before the big show. But he's retired?"

"Indeed, magnificently."

"He was as brilliant as everyone claimed?"

"You know as well as anyone that I swore to give no details of his death—for that knowledge belongs to myself and his patron. But I'm sure you can surmise the truth well enough."

"Then I suppose I should congratulate you, master—"

"Wilco."

"Master Wilco, the Exquisite Corpse! And I suspect that you've come looking for an apprentice."

At only thirteen, Kay was as good with a wrench as her mother had been with a knife, and as Wilco's imagination blossomed through the years she helped extend and maintain the great leviathan. Back then, she did not yearn for dying, though she understood its ethos well enough. Its delicate artistry and unseen perfections enchanted her like it did everybody else. She was wary, though, of apprenticeship itself. Ought one strive to make each death original and singular? How could she die in the way that suited her if she spent each hour toiling at the whispers of a retired Corpse? Wilco never answered that question properly, and indeed it seemed to disturb him. In time, once they left her village, she learned not to ask.

As Wilco stood above the lamplit crowd, preparing for the show, Kay adjusted the bolts of each arm precisely, but not perfectly, having found long ago the degree to which the perfection of the details harmed the perfection of the whole. It was she who designed the mechanism that switched from the loose strings of exhibition shows to the taught razors of their testing. Not a master, she stayed in the background, and did not cultivate the loud dress and personality of a typical Corpse, who drew crowds as much with the drama of their lives as with the execution of their spectacle.

"It's as much an act as death is," said the famous Corpse, Francesca, in her memoire. "I wear the drapery and my long hair, the bright colours and the sequins, the gold and gems, as an emblem of my craft. Death is a performance art, and like a play its authenticity derives from the presentation as much as the act."

Kay had met Francesca, briefly, at a banquet held on the eve of her retirement, and had shaken her nervous hands beneath the tableau of her smiling face. Her obsidian hair and speckled gloves, typically radiant, made the indulgence of the conversation clear. Kay's attire—logical, restricted, tight—inscribed her as beneath such wisdom, not yet an artist, not yet a Corpse creating their own death.

"What did you mean, in your book, when you said that the finery, the celebrity, was as much an act as dying is?"

"Why, dear, how could it not be?"

"I've seen your exhibitions: your death is complicated, acrobatic. That you can do it at all is magnificent, but to attempt it in such irrational attire—?"

"Oh, you see, I thought the same thing when I was an apprentice. You only get one chance at the real thing, right?

Only one true performance, and everything else is just rehearsal and fundraising. I understand that, really. I must seem like a fool to you, perfecting my act for years just to risk slipping on a piece of fabric."

"Yes, exactly. Why fuss with all of this?"

"For some I guess it would be better not to. That was how things were back in the day, like when my old master's master lived and practiced in the court of a duke, hidden from all eyes in his studio, what back then they called a tomb. But the show's not just for the patrons anymore. I practice as much for my fans, and not least because they pay the larger part of my income."

"But they'll never get to see the final show. Just decades of works in progress."

"Exactly, dear. They only get to see a shadow of the real thing—but they do get to see me. And so I figure, why not put in a little extra work to make that me as interesting to them as possible? I would sooner cease trading in the glamour of the act as I would the stories we share of successful deaths, their glory and unseen perfection which is all the common people ever get."

Outsiders never really know how a retirement goes, but rumours always get out, sometimes intentionally. It was said that, when the act was over, Francesca's patron crumbled to the floor and wept at the beauty of her dissected limbs and hands, the bloodstain ebbing from her dress growing like a lattice through the carefully assembled layers—fabric guiding gore, producing art.

Wilco, on his balcony, took the purple ascot from his neck, as he always did, and kissed it. Throwing it to the crowd he pointed vaguely down and shouted, "For that young lady there! I've had my eye on you all night." And he could hear the people cheering. Below him, the red-dyed strings shivered in the wind. His tumble would bleed them white, marking with crimson the lifelines of his death. Kay came up from her inspection, reporting that not all was well.

"The leftmost arm on layer four is not where it should be. I can't get it to reset from performance to exhibition. Its string is still too tight, and could still cut you."

Wilco, his face serene and careful, glanced down to the crowd, their cries and laughter climbing up through the air as though on a stairway, reaching spectrally to touch his face.

"It'll be fine," he said. "This isn't the real thing, no matter what that arm or the audience thinks. I'm in control. We're doing it."

A master does not retire until they are confident that their death has been perfected and that their apprentice is prepared to take their spot. Though patrons might complain and fume about delays, this rule was among the few remaining that were sacred, so not even the most craven Corpses would execute their deaths too early. The death of Wilco's master was not even a week old when he arrived in Kay's village doing exhibitions, practicing, and attempting to entice any child crafty and sincere enough to learn the art of death. A prodigy who had worked for a prodigy, he was among the youngest masters in history. Now he was the oldest one left.

Though some in the village thought performance vulgar, Kay's parents were enthralled with the notion of their daughter up on a stage, a master like themselves, and of a similar art. She had three older siblings, so would never inherit the family business, and with the lack of direction came a lack of mastery, the absence of a drive towards perfection. Yet Wilco could see a glimmer of a spark in her, and so to stay on her parents' good side began to buy his pigs from them.

"What was it like, apprenticing to the great Sigismund?" Kay's mother asked one day.

"I learned a great deal, though of course as most apprentices complain I had little time to experiment with my own ideas. But he taught me such great care, such great perfectionism, that I scarcely doubt I got the worst of the deal. Given time, I expect that my death shall be as great as his was—greater even."

"But first you need to find an apprentice."

"Indeed. The work is too great for one person, and I am duty-bound to pass on what I know."

"Our daughter, Kay, I think, has taken an interest in you."

"And I think she would make an excellent Corpse. Though I sense some worry in you."

"Yes. It is a shame, but I've never been able to go to the city and see a Corpse perform, so you'll forgive my hesitation."

"Not at all. And think: when I retire, you will never hear the end of her. Few parents learn as much of their children as they do the celebrities in the papers. How much better will you know your daughter once she puts on her master's cape?"

Stepping down the ladder but still high above the buildings and the crowd, Kay's eyes hooked upon a second gathering in the distance, people who had skipped out on Wilco's exhibition to see a convict guillotined in the city square. She had been taught to scoff at such artless pseudo-deaths, such amateurish spectacle, yet the comporture of the convict held her gaze. The masked executioner, himself a convict staying his demise for the duration of his labour, rose grandstanding in front of the guillotine in his gaudy, tasselled mask, bringing the crowd to frenzy. Pushed forward to the apparatus, the convict did not struggle, though something in the spirit of him did, a quiver no less real because implied. As the guillotine came shut, a roar went out among the blood-dimmed crowd, who cheered the head as it was held aloft. From her lonely angle, high on the tower, Kay could see the faceless body slump into the ground, its tableau not set up for her, not made for anyone at all.

Before Kay could continue her climb down from the balcony, Wilco called her back up.

"I changed my mind," he said, "so tell the people below to wait just a few minutes more. I'll be fixing that arm myself. Sigismund would not approve, I realized, if I let a machine go telling me what to do."

Kay descended quickly and, as apprentices traditionally did, joined the assembled crowd at its front. In a sense she was an apprentice spectator as much as an apprentice Corpse, taking the role of the absent patron for whose eyes the work was done. Wilco's would be the only death, besides her own, that she was permitted to experience. Only a patron like Carmillo, who had funded Sigismund and Wilco and had agreed, even in his advanced age, to fund Kay as well, would spectate more than one.

Or would he? Kay wondered. Perhaps if he funded other Corpses she had never heard of. Not long after Kay had joined Wilco and the two of them ventured on a wagon from Kay's village to the studio Carmillo rented for them near the square in the city's core, Wilco took Kay out to his favourite social club to teach her how to drink.

"One must learn to be charming even in the most difficult of times," he said as he filled their glasses. "For performing a death, I can say from experience, is even more uncomfortable than whiskey." Kay nipped at the edges of her glass and tried to make the first drink last all night.

The evening went on and Wilco, the toast of the crowd, a Corpse among his people, slowly became sullen and withdrawn. Nursing his whiskey neat, just before last call, he confided something quietly in Kay's ear:

"Sigismund," he said, "never completed his death. I saw it myself. He said he could not face the agony, that he knew he would lose his composure when the wires began to cut. Something of the realness of it stung him. He said he would dishonour his master and the art if he lost his dignity as he performed. So, panicking, he took a poison, and stepped out to the parapet. Expiring on his feet, he fell and was dismembered, artlessly."

Shocked, Kay stayed silent as Wilco wept into her ear.

"I had such plans back then, such plans! But then with this disaster, the pattern of my master's death became my life. That is why we must be perfect, Kay! We owe it to him, to Carmillo. He has paid so much for a death, even took me in when my master failed. A second chance he gave to me—and a clean slate to you. The patrons always claw back money when a death has failed, but not him! Never him." He knocked his whiskey back. "I feel like a cadaver in a morgue, bloated and ugly. I wish Sigismund was still here."

They never spoke of the matter again. Kay was always afraid to bring it up.

Over their years together the death they planned was like a flower growing atop Sigismund's grave. Kay's ideas, and they were many, stayed dormant in her notes. The basic notion of the wires and the arms they borrowed and enhanced, sketching on their diagrams the disintegration of Wilco's body from the cuts. His fingers blooming like a rose, his skin flayed off by gravity, the iridescent splatter of his blood, until his body landed on its feet, for a moment seeming as though still alive, until it fell into the ground, descending from a body into meat.

Among the people in the exhibition crowd, Kay could hear the murmurs of boredom and frustration as they watched Wilco, prancing like an acrobat, climb down the arms to fidget with the gears. He opened the contraption, tightened something, tightened it again, and then satisfied he climbed back up to his parapet and readied for his leap.

To cheers he fell and through the first three layers bounded acrobatically between the strings, the dye inscribing all their plans across his body. Kay had always thought the lines made him look just like the diagram pinned up in her parents' butcher shop, which marked out the different cuts of beef.

Kay turned her eyes back to observe the crowd and at that moment heard a crack. Looking again, she saw Wilco's body shrouded in his cape, hidden, falling rudely now below the shattered arm of layer four. His uncontrolled momentum sent the mechanism into frenzied spins. Instinctively she put her hands up to her eyes before he hit the cobblestones below.

As Wilco, just in case, had told her to, she ran to his remains and, after pretending to check for a pulse, proclaimed that he was injured but alive. His great cape kept his blood obscured until she whisked him out of sight. Weeks later they put out an ad in all the papers, celebrating the successful retirement of an exalted Corpse.

Soon after, Carmillo passed away, and Kay received a package wrapped in Wilco's cape. In his will, to provide entertainment for his son, Carmillo left Kay the blueprint of the balcony and a pension that would fund her art—one worth to roughly half of what Wilco had received.

## ACKNOWLEDGEMENTS

These stories were written over a period of about ten years, and as such benefit from the many friends and colleagues who I have known in that time—far too great a debt for me to properly acknowledge here. They were written in the gaps between a PhD thesis, a poetry collection, journalism, book reviews, academic articles, and the drafts of multiple novels, and so have in my eyes the wounded scrappy preciousness of a stray cat. To list only a handful of especially notable critics, friends, co-conspirators, and colleagues, I would like to extend my deepest thanks to Robert Alexander, Gary Barwin, Rohama Bassett, Gregory Betts, Lindsay Cahill, David Carlton, Tim Conley, Adam Dickinson, Craig Dodman, Ed Edmonds, Kevin Goodwin, Davis Hoye, David Hubert, Ian Hynd, Fred King, Nahmi Lee, Phillip Luckhardt, Riley McDonald, Phil Miletic, Allan Pero, Eric Schmaltz, Tom Stuart, Natalie Trevino, Terry Trowbridge, Natasha Tuskovich, and Jade Wallace—all of whom at different times lent criticism, suggestions, companionship, or encouragement without which many of these stories would not have been written, or at the very least would not be as good.

All mistakes and omissions are the responsibility of the author, whoever the heck that is.

Several of these stories have appeared, sometimes in different forms and under different titles, in various literary journals. They are: "The Forever Pit" (as "Falling Action") in *Popshot Magazine* 8 (2012) with an illustration by Shaun Lynch, "Unconditional Love" in *The Dalhousie Review* 91.1/2 (2012), "Lone and Level Sands" in *The Other Herald* 54 (2014), "Once Again" in *The Dalhousie Review* 96.1 (2016), and "The Fox Beneath the Statue" in *The Puritan* 37 (2017).